Something Happened Yesterday

Also by Beryl Bainbridge

Every Man for Himself
The Birthday Boys
The Dressmaker
An Awfully Big Adventure
Harriet Said
The Secret Glass
The Bottle Factory Outing
Sweet William
A Quiet Life
Injury Time
Young Adolf
Another Part of the Wood
Winter Garden
A Weekend With Claude
An English Journey
Mum & Mr. Armitage
Watson's Apology

Something Happened Yesterday

Beryl Bainbridge

Carroll & Graf Publishers, Inc.
New York

First Carroll & Graf edition 1998

Carroll & Graf Publishers, Inc.
19 West 21st Street
New York, NY 10010-6805

Library of Congress Cataloging-in-Publication data
is available.
ISBN: 0-7867-0517-5

Manufactured in the United States of America

Contents

Preface

A few years ago the *Evening Standard* asked me to write a weekly column, something I continued to do for six years. It took me a little time to hit the right note. An article of eight hundred words was thought to be tiring on the reader; far better to break it up into three or four 'bites' on different themes. This I found constricting; once up and running, I saw no good reason to stop until I reached the finishing line. Also, I mistakenly attempted to grapple with so-called burning issues, an undertaking which required so much research, not to mention informed comment, and turned out to be so confusing – since I was playing with language and had no sooner set down one point of view than another contradictory opinion flashed into my mind – that I soon abandoned the notion and wrote instead about things that happened to me during the week. That seemed to be what people wanted anyway.

In the beginning I had to be reminded that I was writing for a *London* audience, something which had slipped my attention, and that articles about Liverpool or the holidays my Auntie Nellie took in Blackpool before the war were unsuitable for a metropolitan newspaper. In order to surmount this restriction – I have never been intrigued by the present or curious about the future – I took as my example the broadcasts of Alistair Cook and embarked in print on a circular ramble, starting and ending with memories of long-gone times and sticking London in the middle.

The authoritarian voice, the ring of confidence, is not for me. I'm not bothered with causes or hard facts; my preoccupation is not with the immediate how and why of the lives we lead, but rather with a raking over of the life we once knew.

Here then is a selection of the articles I wrote. To me, they read like a diary: Charlie and Darling Bertie growing up, their Grandfather returning in the Great Storm, those terrible visits to writing courses, those blushing appearances on radio or telly, those Tuesdays spent round the kitchen table arguing with the cleaner, the secretary and the youngest daughter. For such indulgences, and being paid for it, my heartfelt thanks to Genevieve Cooper and Neil Norman.

B.B.

1. Street carnival

The Albert Street Carnival is now a thing of the past. Over the years sharp traders and second-hand-clothes merchants moved in, none of whom were into contributing a penny of profit towards anything so barmy as the beautification of a street. Ken and John hung up both the frock coat and the lion-tamer's outfit, and that was that. You could say it marked the end of a neighbourly movement, goodwill to all men, that had spilled over from the sixties.

Something happened yesterday – our street's annual carnival. The rain kept off for a whole afternoon. There were stalls and pop groups, hot-dog stands and roundabouts for toddlers. I bought a winter coat for 30p, a quantity of toys and a crucifix. The undoubted hits of the afternoon were the Punch and Judy show and the palmist, in that order. When Mr Punch maltreated the baby the roar of outrage from the infant audience could be heard in Mornington Crescent.

Originally, sixteen years ago to be exact, carnival day evolved out of a desire to beautify the street. A few months before, someone had come along and ripped out the old street lamps and put in those hideous new things. The same sort of vandalism took place in Gloucester Crescent, but there the residents protested so strongly that they were put back the following day. Our street decided that, with the old lamps gone forever, we might at least have a few trees, and the proceeds of that first event went towards buying, and subsequently planting, tasteful saplings along the edges of the pavement. The idea of environmental improvement was abandoned as soon as it was discovered that nobody had taken into account the camber of the road. In no time at all the roots of the trees began to interfere with the drains and the council had to come round and uproot them – the cost came out of the rates – and stuck them back into huge concrete tubs that remain an eyesore.

The only trees that grew properly after that were the ones in front of the Council flats; every summer the occupants disappear behind an impenetrable wall of greenery. On wet nights you can hear plaintive calls for help from the rain forest. For the first ten years of the carnival most of us had young children, and those were the best years. On the Great Day we kept our front doors open and sprinted in and out of each other's houses, and at night we went to a bash at the play-centre. There was a Fathers' race and all the Dads who had abandoned home came back for the afternoon and ran as though they'd never left. When the children grew up, many of us lost interest, though Peter and Rosie, Ken and John – Ken in his frock coat and John in his lion-tamer's outfit – still continued to do sterling work in the interests of the street.

I gave up participating about six years ago, after I was persuaded to be a fortune-teller. I had foolishly mentioned that I knew someone who had a crystal ball and in no time at all I'd promised to perform at the carnival. I tried to practise gazing in the privacy of the home, but even with my glasses on I couldn't see a thing. There wasn't anything to see; it was all just a foggy blur. On the day, disguised behind a moustache and wearing a nightie and a Davy Crockett hat, I was installed in the gutter in a sort of rickety wigwam half-way down the street. I had a little card table on which to place the tool of my trade. I was crouched there, listening to the opening ceremony – the mayor of Camden was holding forth from a balcony – when the wigwam fell over. Rescued, and settled again, I was wiping the mud from my crystal ball when I was astonished to see little lines and symbols appearing as if by magic within its milky depths. Heartened, I opened my wigwam for business and began gazing. No sooner had my first customers, a man and a woman, put their money on the table than I 'saw' two wiggly lines, several black dots and a sort of spider's web. It became clear that the lines were tyre marks and the black spots were

'I see tyre-marks in the sand.'

various boxes strung out across the snow. 'I see a vast open plain,' I said. 'And some sort of breakdown. Things have had to be abandoned.'

'Good God,' said the girl. Apparently they'd recently been to the Sahara by jeep and had a terrible time. When they went out I could hear them telling everyone that the fortune-teller was amazing. A queue formed. I quite enjoyed myself, at first. It was simple once I'd got the hang of it, even though the wiggly lines never altered and the spider's web stayed in the same place. It was all a matter of observation. Nicotine stains on the fingers pointed to a death-wish, bloodshot eyes noted a dependency on the bottle, nervous laughter was a sure sign of inferiority.

I did make a mistake with a lad who came in with a scar above his eye. I said he'd had an accident as a child. 'Something to do with a bus,' I murmured, gazing at my tyre tracks. He was scornful. He said I was miles off; his dad had hit him over the head with a car handle.

And then an old woman came in, someone who was known locally as Betty the Bins because she was always foraging for old clothes. She'd been in the district for years and had once played the ukulele on talent nights at the Princess Beatrice pub. I found myself telling her she'd not had much of a life.

'You're right,' she said. 'You're bloody right.'

'You've never had it easy,' I said. 'Not even as a child.'

'No,' she sniffed. 'I never.'

I told her that her life had been one long search for something, and that I wished I could see something good happening to her in the future. I was about to turn the two wiggly lines into a pools coupon, but before I could say a word she cried out, 'But you bloody can't, can you?' and stood up so violently that the wigwam collapsed again.

I went home after that. I didn't need a crystal ball to see I'd overstepped the mark.

2. Film heroes

This piece was prompted by something that happened in the High Street. A television crew was filming one of those dramas in which some swine was required to belt a woman in the stomach. A passer-by, unaware that the victim was being paid to be attacked, grappled with her opponent, at which a member of the crew wrestled him to the ground and sat on him.

I went to the pictures the other evening and spent a good part of the time with my eyes shut. No, it wasn't *The Fly*, but something called *Salvador*.

In my early days of cinema-going, mostly on Saturday afternoons at the Palace in Southport, films were very different. If it was a peacetime film, everyone in it wore evening dress and chain-smoked, except when they were dancing on the table tops. A hero who behaved badly, cheated at cards or spoke roughly to a lady was quickly sorted out. If he didn't apologise and see the error of his ways he came to a bad end. American wartime films sometimes had a hero who came home on furlough in a depressed state and twitched a lot. 'Don't you go messing about, sugar,' he'd say, slapping the face of the girl next door, but that was all right because she was his sweetheart and he was in the grip of passion. When he died, on screen, he talked a lot about Momma and left his baseball bat to his kid brother.

If it was an English war film, the hero went home on leave either to a mansion in the country – the butler always opened the door and said, 'Why, Master Charles, I'd hardly have known you' – or to a very smart house in Mayfair with a huge bowl of flowers in the hall. Here Master Charles usually said, 'Is my mother in?', and ran up the stairs laughing. Master Charles had obviously never hit anything in his life, except a cricket ball into the slips. One was left with two very strong impressions: only the rich could be heroic, and nobody wealthy ever set foot downstairs unless they were going out.

Minor characters came from the working classes. They were either poor but honest, salt of the earth and all that, slipping from the life raft so as not to be a burden, giving up the only available parachute, or else cowards, barmaids and spivs.

More often than not, Master Charles ran into flak over Germany on his last mission, just after announcing that the sky was as smooth as a cricket pitch, and crashed off screen. Months later a young lady called either Joan or Ann turned up in Mayfair and declared she was pregnant. She was invariably one of the poor-but-honest sort, rather refined, as the salt of the earth needs to be if it wants to be used, and never motivated by money. All that Joan/Ann was really after was a fitting nest for her child.

When she broke the news, Charles's father, before rushing off to put the baby's name down for Eton, had to remind Charles's mother that the old world had gone forever. She knew, of course, without being told, and she didn't bat an eyelid. Nor was she ever seen to shed a tear at the death of her son. She would have thought it vulgar to make a public show of grief.

Such reticence does indeed appear to have gone forever, booted out by television. Take the first reports last week of the sinking of the cross-Channel ferry, and those early interviews with survivors.

'It turned over ... people were screaming ... there were children floating about,' a girl sobbed.

'And what did you feel at such a sight?' asked the interviewer.

And later, Mr Kinnock and Dr Owen were dragged in and interrogated as to their emotions on hearing the news. Naturally, they were both 'devastated'. As neither of them had relations on board I can't see why they were asked. Besides, only a madman or a depressive would reply that he couldn't care less. I can't make up my mind whether they were wheeled on to prove that politicians have the right attitudes, or because television is beginning to fear that the rest of us, subjected to constant and possibly numbing screen images, are no longer capable of responding correctly to death and disaster.

Which brings me back to the film *Salvador* in which the main character was a foul-mouthed, foul-living news photographer, who, when he wasn't drunk or in a whore-house, spent his time clambering over a rubbish tip taking shots of mutilated corpses. The film itself was no doubt worthwhile, bringing to our notice as it did the suffering which continues to exist in Central America, but as a hero the photographer was a revelation, particularly in his attitude to women. After all, there's nothing a true woman likes better than to be humped in a hammock by an unshaven, unwashed lout while the bombs are falling and the baby is crying under the table.

No clue was given about what sort of background our hero came from, but he did seem to be on nodding terms with quite a few generals and senators, all of whom were equally brutal towards women,and it's comforting to think that by now, in real life, the whole piggy bunch of them would have succumbed to AIDS.

It's an interesting phenomenon, this modern leading character who achieves heroic stature by default, who must be seen to be wallowing in mud, so to speak, before reaching for the stars, and whose dying words must invariably be four-letter ones. Are we to understand that this is realism, the way things really are and have always been, and that the old breed of hero, Captain Scott on his way to the Pole, Baden-Powell at Mafeking, were no different? I hope not, if only for the sake of Master Charles's mother.

3. History of spanking

This was inspired by a book just issued by my publishers. The lady rumoured to wear a hairy vest was a relation of mine who in fact was known to wear white gloves in bed. One has to be very careful; libel cases can land one in the poor-house.

It has been a punitive week, one way and another, what with the arrest of the MP accused of spanking and that medical chap claiming that a whipping a day is more beneficial than an apple.

The gullibility of some people is extraordinary. Fancy trotting along to morning surgery with a head cold and being told to bend over for six of the best – though of course it might take one's mind off the snuffles. You'd have thought, what with all the amateur, instant psychology rolling around on television, that the person in the street would smell a rat immediately, or at least think something was up, if only his suspicions. And then to be sworn at into the bargain!

'But if ye be without chastisement, whereof all are partakers, then ye are bastards and not sons' (Hebrews, verse 8).

I don't think women are much into spanking – doing it, that is " unless paid, mostly because we prefer being dominated as opposed to dominating. As for being on the receiving end, I have been racking my brains to remember whether it ever happened to me. I have a very dim memory of my mother belabouring me with a slipper for swearing, and I once slapped one of the children for fiddling with an electric light socket, but I don't believe I *enjoyed* either incident.

Now I come to think of it, I do remember there was a lady in our village, living with her brother, who was rumoured to wear a hairy vest all through Lent. And there was a butcher's boy who boasted of doing something unmentionable with sausages, but perhaps that's different. It's also true that comics in my day, the *Dandy* and the *Beano* in particular, were full of drawings of schoolteachers' swishing canes, but one didn't take them seriously. I'm convinced that if any unfortunate teacher, let alone a kinky old gentleman, had attempted to flog me, I would have risen up at the first touch of the rod and throttled him, but then I never had the benefit of a public school education.

I don't even understand the difference between sadism and masochism. To my mind, they seem to end up as the same thing. I admit to masochistic tendencies – surely another of those instances when it is better to receive than to give – in that I quite enjoy being put down, or put upon, if only because it gives me pleasure to point out how unfairly I am being treated. Do take the remaining crust of bread, I insist, the only tomato, the last dregs in the whisky bottle. Do walk all over me, I suggest. After a decent interval of anything up to twenty years, I bring the matter up.

'That tomato,' I reminisce, 'do you remember? I've never forgotten the way you munched upon it, the way the pips caught in your teeth. It was raining, and your mother was there wearing a yellow dress. Have that tomato, dear, I said, and you did.'

This sort of thing obviously makes me a sadist, which is why I'm confused. As far as I'm aware I have never felt sadistic except once, and that was when the cat did a whoopsie on the landing carpet. I ran all over the house calling it rude names and found it sitting on the bathroom mat. I opened the back door and told it to get out, but it wouldn't budge. In the end I picked it up, swollen with rage (me, I mean), and hurled it out into the back yard. To this day I can hear its banshee cry of protest, its howl of anguish, as I trapped its tail in the door. The memory still makes me miserable, which is surely masochistic.

Be that as it may, I have been doing a little reading on the subject of spanking, and am amazed, as both Richard II and Frankie Howerd were apt to exclaim, at my findings. For instance, did you know that the first coherent attempt to explain flagellation as a sexual stimulant was made in the seventeenth century by a Doctor Meibom? Now there's a name to conjure with. And did you know that Swinburne, that fellow who plagiarised the immortal Biblical line 'By the waters of Babylon we sat down and wept', also wrote something called 'Arthur's Flogging', the last three lines of which read:

With piteous eyes uplifted, the poor boy
Just faltered, 'Please, sir', and could
  get no farther.
Again, that voice, 'Take down your trousers, Arthur.'

Poor old Swinburne was beaten so often when he was at Eton that in later life he thought about little else.

Mr Gladstone wasn't much better – 'bottom mad' he was called – but then his headmaster at Eton was that daddy of all beaters, the notorious *plagosus Orbilius* Dr Keate – Flogging Keate, as he was known. Perhaps we shouldn't be surprised to learn that Gladstone, returning from one of his 'charitable' visits to the haunts of 'fallen women', was in the habit of flagellating himself. No wonder that, on becoming Prime Minister, he recorded in his diary the following thoughts: 'I ascend a steepening path, with a burden ever gathering weight. The Almighty seems to sustain and spare me for some purpose of his own, deeply unworthy as I know myself to be. Glory be to his name.' Disraeli, on attaining the same office, merely remarked, 'I have climbed to the top of the greasy pole.' All the same, I think, on balance, that Gladstone was a good egg. A man who came from Liverpool can't be all bad, and he did appoint a Secretary of State who abolished flogging in the Army.

It does put a different complexion on that neighbour's hairy vest, and if only we'd concentrated on such things at school, rather than on the details of that boring old Reform Bill, we might have found history more fundamentally absorbing.

I've also discovered that as late as 1968 there was a gentleman in Bognor Regis who did a brisk trade in selling canes by post. He sold more than 4,000 in under two years, and considered moving to a leafier part of the countryside because he was running out of trees.

'Some of the most famous people in the land,' he confided, 'cutting across all social classes, have used my canes. They are beating a path to my door.'

These fascinating items of information, should you be interested, come from a remarkable book *The English Vice*, written by Ian Gibson, which was brought to my attention by a masterly publisher's advert in the *Times Literary Supplement* which announced: 'Coming at last in soft back, the history of spanking at a price that will really hurt.'

4. Vale of tears

I did meet this lonely soul in a café. She depressed me. The bits about Tulsa are true, but happened in another context. It was salutary, though not surprising, to read the other day that the Evangelical dreams of Oral Roberts have, like golden lads and lasses, come to dust.

You don't really have to go anywhere to get anywhere. This somewhat abstract remark is prompted by what happened to me last week, when, intending to see the exhibition of British Art at the Academy, I ended up on foot in Piccadilly Circus trying in vain to cross the road.

I've passed through Piccadilly in a taxi on numerous occasions but it's been years since I actually walked round it, or attempted to, and I must say I don't appear to have missed much. There are huge holes in the road, and Lillywhite's, which I seem to remember as an imposing enough building, now looks as if it was used on the set of Hitchcock's film *The Birds*.

As I couldn't see a vacant cab I went into a sandwich bar for a cup of coffee and was immediately buttonholed by a young woman from Scotland who pleaded with me not to smoke.

As politely as possible I pointed out the ash-tray, the empty seats at the door, the fog of exhaust fumes that covered the windows in a grey scum.

'It's you I'm thinking of,' she said.

You must admit that these days such kindly concern is somewhat disconcerting: one can never tell what lies behind it. As it turned out, she was just mildly potty and very lonely. She hadn't exchanged a single word with anyone for more than a week and was determined to make up for lost time. Mostly she wanted to talk about God. I did try to steer our chat along less momentous avenues, but she was having none of it. For some reason she took me for an Indian – I can look rather sallow during the winter months – and congratulated me on the admirable way 'my' people disposed of their dead.

Flustered at the assumption, yet taken by an inner vision of my Aunt Nellie floating on a burning raft down the Ganges by way of the river Mersey, I suddenly heard my companion uttering the observation that life was a 'vale of tears' and was instantly transported from India to Tulsa, Oklahoma.

Let me explain this extraordinary leap of continents, albeit in the imagination. Mention of God and death had unwittingly reminded me of that wretched, money-oriented evangelist Oral Roberts, who was so much in the news the other week. Preacher Roberts was the fellow who announced on American television that God had told him he would die – 'Come in, Oral, your time is up' – if he didn't raise eight million dollars by last Tuesday. In case any of you are worried, a lot of saintly, not to say ignorant, people have already sent him the money and, barring accidents, such as a thunderbolt from on high, he'll live on, running in rude health all the way to the bank.

Now, I've met Oral, or rather travelled in a lift with him, in the Tulsa Hilton Hotel, one night during a convention dinner held for bird-lovers – people who love shooting them, that is. He didn't speak to me, of course, and I wasn't at the dinner, but we stood belly to belly as the lift went up to heaven on the 21st floor where a celestial fountain sprinkled the lobby. He was quite a reserved-looking man, unlike his fellow ornithologists who sported entire birds' heads, bloody feathers and all, stuffed in to the bands of their Stetson hats.

Later that night, on telly, there he was in a nice white suit asking for money. 'No matter how little you can give,' he said. 'God will personally thank you.' On enquiring about him, I was told he owned practically all the television networks, a university and a hospital. He was a millionaire, possibly a double one, and he'd made his money out of God. By contrast, the other citizens of Tulsa had made theirs out of oil, which may or may not be more honourable.

Which brings me to the vale, or rather the trail, of tears, signifying the route taken by the dispossessed Indians who were driven from their home lands and resettled in a corner of Oklahoma. The new lands were given to them legally, signed and sealed, and it was a bit of a shock to all concerned, the givers and the receivers, to discover years later, long after the ink had dried, that there was oil in them there fields.

Tulsa itself, it seemed to me, was not so much a place as an architect's model; a collection of skyscrapers, white as paper, set down in the wilderness. By day the tumbleweed bowled across the scorched earth, and at night the horizon was ringed with oil stacks flaring like candles on a cake.

I was taken to a museum in the middle of nowhere filled with Indian art and artefacts, and circling a totem pole I found myself stalking Henry Kissinger. (He didn't talk to me either.) He read aloud a speech written on parchment by Chief Seattle in 1855 – a raging, mournful protest at the land being taken from his people:

'At night when the streets of your cities are silent and you think them deserted, they will throng with the returning hosts that once filled them and still love this beautiful land. The white man will never be alone.'

Later that night, in the small hours, I was woken by an eerie wailing and thought it was the braves come back to claim their birthright, but it was only the war-whoop of a freight train as it crossed the intersection of Main Street and rolled on into the darkness.

'I've got to get out of my room by the end of the week,' said the girl from Scotland. She didn't ask me if I knew of anywhere, and when I got up to leave I thought of putting a fiver under my saucer, but she was so vague I didn't think she'd spot it and in any case it was hardly a deposit on a place to live.

I set off on my own particular trail of tears and crossed Piccadilly Circus. They were still digging. I suppose it's another complex for offices, though it could be the drains. Then again, perhaps they've struck oil.

Footnote. Dear Mr Crighton, I think there's been a misunderstanding. When I wrote my article on screen heroes, in which I suggested that girls named Joan or Ann were likely to arrive on Master Charles's doorstep with a bun in the oven, I had no intention of implying that all girls with such names ended up in a delicate condition without the benefit of wedlock. If you feel I have offended your wife, then I sincerely apologise. Believe me, I had no idea that Mrs Crichton worked in Mayfair before the war, and as you so rightly say, coming from a strict Methodist family she would not have allowed Master Charles to touch her with a barge pole.

Also, my reference to women liking nothing better than to be humped in a hammock was written tongue in ironic cheek.

5. Self-expression

None of this is made up, not even the extract from the elderly lady's novel, but I confess that appalled as I was – and still am – at the deplorable teaching standards in our schools, I was banging a drum in the interests of education. (The best residential writing school at the moment seems to be the one run by my editor Alice Thomas Ellis at her house in Wales – Trefechan in Powys.

Something happened yesterday. I went to Southampton University to take part in a Literary Festival.

Angelina had blue eyes, a good bust and rippling waves. She threw her eyes round the room and they fell on a young man's tweed trousers ... Angelina sighed.

I wish I could furnish you with more, in particular why those trousers caused Angelina such sorrow, but the elderly lady who showed me these tantalising lines hadn't got any further with her novel and was hoping I might be of help.

'Is it a love story?' I asked.

'It could be,' she said, 'but I'd like someone to die.'

I did think Angelina, having lost those blue peepers in such an abrupt way was a likely candidate, but the author wasn't keen. Angelina was the pivot of the plot.

You have no idea how many thousands of people, up and down the country, spend their spare time writing novels, poetry and radio plays. Indeed, it sometimes seems that the pursuit of self-expression, like snooker, has become a national pastime. Already this year I have attended four such festivals, turned down three, and in November I'm off to Arvon, which isn't so much a Festival as a residential writing course.

Arvon – nothing to do with that lady who keeps ringing at the front door and bringing out samples of lipstick – has two centres, one in Devon and one at Lumb Bank, Yorkshire. In both places, almost every week of the year, five-day courses are held for aspiring writers, tutored by established authors. There are no rules for entry, except that one should be over sixteen and if you don't want to write anything down or are too shy to show anybody what you have already done, then you can just take to your bed, or the pub, or go walking in the beautiful countryside.

There wasn't much time for walking in Southampton, unless it was from one room to another to receive hints on this or that branch of writing, and quite a few participants fell by the wayside, snoring in armchairs, such was the pace of the day.

In the old days, of course, it was the Labour Party who encouraged such goings on – self-improvement that is, not snoring. The Working-Men's Colleges, the Left-Wing Book Clubs, the Workers' Educational Association classes all sprang from a belief that poverty was as much a matter of mind as of pocket.

I can't understand why the Labour Party of today doesn't go on more about education – I mean about the value of it rather than how much it costs. If things go on as they are, one wonders where the future Labour ministers, and Tory Prime Ministers for that matter, seeing Mrs T was a grammar-school girl, are going to come from.

Think of Mrs T, Mr Kinnock and Mr Hattersley suddenly turned into little lads and lasses and subjected to either the primary or the comprehensive school. In the first instance they would be engaged full-time in learning how to swim in pyjamas – always supposing they owned anything so frivolous – how to care for hamsters and how not to run a fire station.

In the second – always supposing that by this time, out of boredom, they weren't into glue-sniffing – they would be concentrating not on the three Rs but on the two Ss, Safe Sex and Survival, the latter covering everything from the destruction of forests to the demise of the man-eating moth and the humble bumble-bee.

Until we live in a world in which either financial reward or an appreciation of excellence lies in the recognition of such studies, there seems no point to them. Unfortunately, children who are products of this admirably free-thinking curriculum, broad in their attitudes, wide in their aptitudes, lovers of humanity and kind to animals, are hardly likely to get into a sixth form, let alone a University. A knowledge of sex and moths is no substitute for Latin, science and maths.

Be that as it may, let us return to Southampton and the vexed question of Angelina. The author, though she had not so far managed to put it onto paper, had the outline of the novel clearly in her head. It would be set in the here and now and centre round a young girl working in a munitions factory who would possibly murder, from the purest of motives, one of three other characters, not including the chap in the hairy trousers. The one singled out to be done in had either seduced and disgraced her or spread unkind stories about her humble origins. He was Satan in human form. Also, and obviously of prime importance, given that the author was approaching her ninetieth year, it must be a short read.

There were a few difficulties to be faced, not least the satisfying portrayal of a modern-day munitions factory. Then of course there was the somewhat extreme reaction to seduction. It was only when I was travelling home on the train that I managed to sort it out.

Angelina had blue eyes, a good bust and rippling waves. She threw her eyes round the room and they fell on a young man's tweed trousers ... Angelina sighed. And then felt horror. Beside the young man sat another man wearing a trilby hat with two horns protruding above its brim. There was no mistaking Satan. Lifting a shell from the assembly line she balanced it on her good bust and staggered towards the devil. Just before the shell exploded, she sighed again. If there is any justice, she thought, I shall go up, not down.

6. Aeons ago

Re-reading this, I am amazed to think that Darling Bertie can now belt out a blues number on the saxophone, and that, in spite of its former treatment, the rambling rose has resurrected itself in all its fearsome glory; I now spend valuable time trying, as yet unsuccessfully, to poison the brute. How time flies!

Last year I wasted several months agonising over my garden wall. By that, I don't mean to imply that I hung across it, spread-eagled atop the rough bricks in an embarrassingly martyred pose, simply that I was bothered by its imminent destruction. My neighbour, a gentleman unacquainted with English law, one bright morning in spring instructed his builder, one Seamus, to knock down the party wall at the bottom of what I euphemistically call my garden, i.e. the back yard.

I won't elaborate on the hysterical telephone calls to the Council, the misunderstanding which arose when the said body thought that the outer structural wall of my listed house was being demolished. Nor will I dwell on the contempt with which my complaints were received at the Town Hall when my piping, choirboy tones were immediately recognised as female.

'Pull yourself together,' said the masculine chap on the other end of the wire, as I shrilly gave him a blow-by-blow account of what was happening. 'Ring after the weekend,' he urged, as my wall and its 150-year-old bricks tumbled into my yard and my rambling rose, a wonder of Woolies if ever there was one, bought twelve years before and now ten feet high and twelve feet across, was guillotined, cut down in its prime.

The following morning my solicitor arrived. He attempted, over what was left of the garden wall, to reason with the demolition crew with the sledge hammers. A former public school boy, a man more used to dealing with Horace than Seamus, he resolutely turned the other cheek – Seamus kept offering to knock his block off – and whimsically drew our attention to the wildlife flitting among the debris.

'Oh,' he cried, 'how lovely. Look, another Red Admiral.'

Seamus, neither a sissy nor a lepidopterist, promptly batted the endangered species with the flat of his spade.

It was explained to him by my daughter's young man that a wall is not always just a wall. In this particular case it symbolised the boundary of somebody's space, imitated the wider, cosmic condition.

'Dear God,' said Seamus, as well he might.

I had forgotten all about the blessed wall, now rebuilt and so much rubble under the bridge, until two days ago, when, it being half term, I took my grandchildren, Charlie and Darling Bertie, on an outing to the Planetarium and Madame Tussauds. The waxworks were a great success – Mrs T and the Royal Family being favourite – as was the Chamber of Horrors, though we went through it somewhat briskly. 'What's that lady doing?' asked Bertie. 'Having a nice splash,' said his mother brightly as we whipped past a Bride in the Bath desperately blowing bubbles.

At the entrance to the Planetarium there was a notice to the effect that anyone under five was unwelcome. Darling Bertie is four and looks like an undernourished three-year-old, so we didn't mention him and he ran under the counter and got in for free. We had to wait for the next performance to begin; neither child seemed shaken by the achievements of Newton or Galileo. They hung about the gift shop, wailing for stars and globes that lit up in the dark. Once they were seated beneath the dome, a small crisis arose when Granny, thoughtfully attempting to prepare them for the treat in store, foolishly mentioned the word 'galaxy'. It took some time to pacify Darling Bertie who refused to believe that there wasn't a sweetie shop on the premises. Fortunately the lights began to dim and we persuaded him that the day had gone very fast and wasn't he a lucky little boy to be up in the middle of the night?

It's a marvellous show, though I reckon I enjoyed it more than the children. The accompanying narration is a bit plummy, and I can't think why they use the music of someone called Vangelis rather than the spine-chilling chords of Gustav Holst, but those two things apart, the information and the presentation is superb. They have a slight breeze blowing across the auditorium, and the seats are angled backwards to give the effect of making a steep climb in an aircraft, and up above is the night sky. It really does bring out prickles at the back of your neck. Ideally, to achieve perfection, one should be drip-fed with whisky while gazing upwards, but I suppose this would prove expensive. It makes you want to cry, that's the point, but nicely. At the end, a sort of heartbeat thunders around the dome, a sound which the narrator tells us is flashed out, Cole Porter fashion, day and night, night and day, ad infinitum from beyond the stars.

Billions upon billions of aeons ago the heavens looked different from the way they are now. All the stars, planets and galaxies were on one side in a lump, and then there was an enormous explosion, bigger than the detonation of a billion, trillion atom bombs, and everything got shot out in all directions. The heartbeat is the echo of the continuing shock-waves which followed that awsome combustion which rearranged the sky.

I forgot to mention that in the course of my wall going down and coming up again I lost one twenty-fourth of an inch of ground. I measured it, so I know, and fretted over it. All that is now behind me, now I've faced the cosmos. One should be grateful for small mercies. At least my wall is not likely to go bang.

Footnote. Dear Mr R.L. Randall. How kind of you to write and tell me how much you enjoyed my article on whipping, though I fear there may have been a misunderstanding on your part. Nowhere in my piece did I mention that I approved of corporal punishment; indeed, looking through my files it is clear that I stressed my abhorrence of such a practice. I am also at a loss to know how you should deal with that lady at the DHSS. Are you sure you heard her correctly? Having consulted several young people of my acquaintance who 'sign on', I am assured that it is not normal policy to make such a quaint proposal. I can only suggest that if it happens again you should attempt a citizen's arrest, though I gather this won't be easy owing to maximum security grilles in position at the counters. Finally, I regret I do not have any photographs of my feet. How very interesting about loofahs!

7. Escaping to London

I have to confess that at the time I hadn't much sympathy with Simone, though I didn't let it show. My Mum hadn't been an alcoholic, but I felt there were worse things than drink. Six years on, I feel ashamed. Also, I did want to get in the joke about Dick Whittington.

Something happened yesterday, mainly a television programme called 'In the Same Boat'. All roads, so they say, lead to London Town. I left home for the big city when I was sixteen, taking with me in a carrier bag from Lewis's my Sunday frock, ration book, and a photograph of Rasputin; I had little more than thirty shillings in my mac pocket. Nichola was sixteen when she came to London from Blackpool in the seventies. She took a room in Chelsea. Simone, sixteen in the eighties, popped up the road from Banbury and slept rough in Piccadilly Circus. The three of us met when we all took part in the programme. Television has a lot of daft ideas, but this wasn't one of them and I thought the resulting discussion was jolly interesting.

Nichola's mother had managed rock bands in Blackpool. She was fifteen when Nichola was born. There must have been money in music because Nichola was sent away to boarding school, and when she was sixteen, friction between mother and daughter becoming unbearable, Mum took her to London and found her a room in Chelsea.

Put like that, it may seem a little casual, but there *are* people of sixteen, and I was one of them, who are perfectly capable of managing on their own, and I only wish my own parents had hit on such a satisfactory arrangement, rather than forcing me to run away. Mind you, in the fifties you weren't expected to leave home until you'd walked up the aisle. Anyone who got away before marriage was known to be either potty or in the family way.

Simone's Mum was an alcoholic and Simone came to London because she thought she'd have a 'better chance'. She'd started glue-sniffing in Banbury, but in Piccadilly there was always someone giving away the sort of pills that made you forget the cold and let you feel happy. There wasn't any difficulty in getting hold of the 'stuff'. One bloke had a dodgy doctor and he shared things out. To get money some girls drifted into prostitution, but Simone had preferred begging. The drugs had helped with her problems, though sometimes she had written poems and that had made her feel good too. She didn't regret anything, except that if she'd had a better education she would find it easier to write things down, to express her thoughts.

I hadn't heard of drugs in the fifties, and Nichola had rejected them after knowing musicians in Blackpool who had died from overdoses, so neither of us could match Simone's experience. Nichola had got high in Chelsea from drinking sherry from the wood, and I had once heard church bells ringing in Marble Arch from being given a glass of gin at a Moral Rearmament Meeting (what on earth was *that* about?), and both of us agreed that we had felt more or less permanently exhilarated just from being away from home.

Our attitudes, then, to sex seemed much the same, even if we used different words, different excuses. Nichola had done 'it' because otherwise you were thought frigid or a lesbian. Simone had done it for the same reasons and because everyone needs affection whether they be 16 or 160. Actually she put the blocks on at 60, which I personally feel is a bit early. I didn't know about lesbians and I imagined frigidity had more to do with a chap's ineptitude than a maiden's psychosis, so I mostly did 'it' out of politeness – it was rude to say no.

So there we were in the studio, the three of us, separated by time and opportunity. Nichola, now managing director of a highly successful communications business, had lived on £6 a week, worn flared trousers and gone to college during Mr Heath's term of office. Simone, who now has a job looking after children, had dyed her hair green, received next to no education and existed on handouts during Mrs Thatcher's reign. As for me, in my duster coat, my wedge-heeled shoes, my belief that saying 'thank you' and 'please' guaranteed me a place in Heaven, I had arrived in London when Mr Attlee was about to depart and Mr Churchill to return. I worked in a cinema in Tottenham Court Road and saw *Cyrano de Bergerac* 37 times and still can't remember the plot. When I lost the job I went by trolley car every Friday morning from Hampstead to Islington to collect my fifteen shillings dole, and afterwards, in a café near Collins' Music Hall, I had my only breakfast of the week: fried bread, egg, sausage and tomato. I remember that all right. On the wall across the street, Tilly the Tassel Queen, her outstanding bosom now possibly twirled to dust, looked down from her poster.

I once saw the pantomime *Dick Whittington* – famous for the heart-felt line, 'Five miles to London and still no Dick' – with that great principal boy Dorothy Ward in the leading role. Her stick over her shoulder and that huge moggie lolloping behind, she sang a song about the streets of London being paved with gold. I think they *were* for me and Nichola. At least we found what we wanted. For Simone it was different, hers was a leaky boat.

That she didn't drown says more for the buoyancy of the human spirit than the ship-shape condition of our present society.

8. Exercise

My Mum is long since dead, but I did have that argument with the Refuse Department, while she lived, about burials in backyards. She died up North and is now lying on top of my Dad, a fate which, in life, she would have regarded as worse than death.

I have been reading recently about a splendid man called Joseph Williamson, known in his time as the King of Edge Hill, who lived in Mason Street, Liverpool, in the early part of the nineteenth century. He was a curious-tempered fellow, who never seemed so happy as when he was grubbing under the surface of the earth. He excavated the street in which he lived – he happened to own it – and when Stephenson's railway navvies were digging out the underground tunnel between Edge Hill and Lime Street station he suddenly burst through the rock wearing corduroy breeches and carrying a pickaxe. He said burrowing was great sport and very good for the muscles.

I mention the deceased Mr Williamson because of late I've been worried that I don't get enough exercise. I used to go to the local baths, but I got fed up with the interference of life-guards who would keep trying to teach me the basic strokes. I've never had the slightest desire to swim under my own steam, if you follow me, being perfectly happy with water-wings, and it was irritating having to pretend I was grateful for instruction. In the end I hinted that I suffered from a malignant disease of the spine – which only made things worse because then they kept rushing up and down along the sides of the pool, presumably ready to plunge in to save me from sinking.

For a while I played tennis with my friend Glenn, but we never got the hang of it. We were both good at serving and

Plenty of room for Mother in the back yard.

duffers at returning. It was a bit limiting, and one spent so much time ferreting for balls in the bushes that there was ample time to get through a packet of ciggies. I don't own a car and in theory I should walk a lot – but then, I don't go out much. I'm also running a one-woman youth opportunity scheme which means I don't scrub the step any more or go shopping. I employ two cleaners, one of whom is my daughter, a secretary and a handyman. As the latter happens to be my son he often leaves in a huff in the middle of some improvement. The second cleaner, known since a toddler, and to all intents and purposes one of the family, invariably becomes tired and emotional half way through the afternoon and, duster in fist, passes out on the top landing. It would not be stretching the truth too far to observe that the only bit of me that gets regular exercise is my right arm which is constantly engaged in working my hand to write out cheques.

The one avenue, or rather square, left to me is my backyard. Here I can plant and dig, bend and squat, tote that barge and lift that weed to my heart's content. At least I could until this week when it became obvious that there wasn't an inch of soil left uncultivated. There are bush roses, wild buttercups, blue things and pink things, ferns sprouting from the brickwork of the wall, poppies popping up like overblown cabbages, all leaf and no flower, some shrub that has white blossom, sweet-peas, pansies, and a lot of dandelions which are now in a he-loves-me-he-loves-me-not condition, poised to travel for miles. There is also a hole, behind a sycamore stump, which belongs to Darling Bertie. It's a sort of archaeology site, being the burial ground of at least four rabbits, three hamsters and as many cats. Bertie digs the bones up from time to time and takes them to school for the infants' nature table.

Many years ago, when my Mum was staying with me, we heard a play on the wireless about a man who buried his wife in the back garden. My mother said it was against the law, and I argued that plays had to be accurate and were always well researched. I rang up the Citizens' Advice Bureau to prove my point, inquiring what forms would be needed in order to bury my Mum in the backyard, and the lady on the other end of the line said I didn't have to go to such lengths and could apply for a funeral grant. When I said I didn't want one she grew hysterical – my mother wasn't exactly calm – and ordered me to contact the refuse department. However, that's another story.

I'm no good at arithmetic so I can't tell you the exact measurements of my garden, but it might fit into an average-sized bathroom. Indeed, in my more lucid intervals, I have day-dreamed of turning my patch into a heated swimming pool, covered by a glass dome, with an aperture beneath my kitchen window through which I could dive, fortified with water-wings, rubber ring, hip-flask and inflatable vest, into the water. This last scheme, being expensive to execute, remains in the fantasy stage.

Anyway, this Monday, frustrated by lack of planting space and exercise, I took a hammer to the concrete and tried to beat out another yard or so of border. Within ten minutes I had walloped the first finger of my cheque-writing hand and was hopping up and down in agony. Still, I persevered and managed to hollow out a reasonable sort of trench which I edged with bricks and filled in with earth pinched from next door. It was then that the handyman, watching languidly from an upstairs window, shouted that I needed to drill holes at least six feet down for drainage. I gave up at once.

In the middle of his excavations three of Joseph Williamson's houses subsided without trace. I shall buy a skipping rope instead.

9. Travel

I think this was prompted by Darling Bertie throwing up in a taxi. I thought he was going to die, and it reminded me of the time I took his mother, her brother and my youngest child across Europe. In real life, the latter was suffering from mumps. I still break out into a sweat at the memory of the gentleman passenger, fortunately foreign, who screamed out at me that my toddler was possibly rendering him infertile.

I always become very uneasy at this time of year, on account of holidays. It ought to be easier now that the kids have grown up and the rabbits, the hamsters and the goldfish have died off, but then there's always the garden to worry about.

I notice that Ralph in *Brookside,* who only took four days off in the Lake District, came back to find that Annabelle had neglected to water his tomatoes. Think what could happen in a fortnight. One thing's for sure – if I do go abroad I won't travel by aeroplane. I'm always astonished at the way friends and acquaintances, some of whom claim to suffer from nerves, fly off in all directions at the drop of a hat. I have flown many times, but I've never enjoyed it, not even under sedation. I tell a lie – the time I went to Israel was relatively stress-free – at least for me – as departure was delayed for two hours owing to Mr Callaghan coming in late on Concorde. By the time I'd knocked back the free drinks and my tranquillisers, plus the ones for the return journey, I was relaxed enough to be wheeled to the plane on a luggage trolley.

I haven't been much luckier when travelling by train. My youngest child still has behavioural problems, due to a return journey from Spain during which she was wrapped in a blanket and made to act the part of a babe in arms. She was almost five at the time and big for her age. I had run out of money and all three children were complaining pitifully of dehydration and starvation. We cashed in her ticket, bought provisions, and coerced her into gurgling across Europe in the foetal position.

And then there was the holiday four years later when the older children flew to Greece, and I and the youngest, plus a little friend called Caroline, followed by train. We had been booked onto the Orient Express by a travel firm in the local high street, and there had been great talk of the suite we would have once we boarded at Paris. There would be a loo of one's own, and as France and Italy and Yugoslavia rolled passed our windows a waiter in an immaculate white coat would serve us appetising, if foreign, meals. The children carried little suitcases containing notebooks and crayons and tracing paper, ready to note down the edifying and educational sights with which the journey would abound. I had perfected a few phrases in three languages – 'Thank you so much', 'What time is our connection?' 'What is that interesting citadel/mountain/animal over there?'

The children had nighties and little slippers with pompoms. Oh, the poignancy of it, even after all these years! We never sat down, from the moment we reached Paris to the time we got to Yugoslavia, and that was only because Caroline seemed to be ill. We lay down a lot, or at least the children did, but that was in the corridors. Caroline came from a very nice family who fed her at regular intervals and, though she wasn't really ill, she sort of got peaky as the days went by. At Milan we were put off the train for hours. It was there that we met the dwarf. He was one of a party of migrant Greek workers who sat on a mountain of luggage on the platform.

They were all very kind to us. When the new train came in and everyone fought to get on, they picked the children up bodily and passed them up with the boxes. Then the train started to move. I was running alongside shouting – it wasn't one of my perfected phrases – and the dwarf stuck out his leg for me to hold onto and clamber up and aboard. It was shortly after this that we got our seats, though it was hardly restful because that was the night some men came into the carriage and unscrewed the roof over our heads. They were straddling us, and when they lifted up their arms you could see guns tucked into the tops of their trousers. They were smuggling jeans over the border. Nobody said anything. We all looked straight ahead and pretended not to notice. Needless to say, we flew home. The travel firm settled out of court. Thinking about it, perhaps it would have been fairer to sue Agatha Christie.

Something happened yesterday which confirms the dangers of travel, even by taxi. Darling Bertie fell on his head in the school playground and came home drowsy. When we got to the doctor's door he woke up and refused to go inside. He was strong enough to kick out in all directions. So we flagged a passing taxi and made for home again. It was very hot and the driver was very irate. He kept complaining about tuppence-ha'penny jobs and the traffic. It's true, the traffic was terrible, and he kept moaning and thumping the wheel with his fists. We were nearly home when Bertie suddenly rolled his eyes and threw up. The driver almost had a heart attack. We ordered him to return at once to the surgery. On the way I gave him a little lecture on stress and how he must deep breathe. When he arrived and he saw the state of his cab, far from following my advice he almost stopped breathing altogether. He had to sit on the kerb. All in all, it's advisable not to use any form of transport except legs. I think I'll buy an exercise bike and travel safely in my own home.

10. Opera

The night before I went to the opera the children's father announced his intention of winging his way across the globe after an absence of sixteen years. It seemed to me that this was a plot worthy of opera.

Odd, isn't it, how events in one's life link up in the most extraordinary way? This week I received a telegram, was taken to the opera and went to the opening of an art exhibition. I grant you the last two things are similar, being of a cultural nature, but I haven't set eyes on a telegram since the GPO did away with those telegraph boys in the little hats and the Sam Browne belts. Nor can I claim to know a lot about opera, having seen but three before: the first in Liverpool, where Kirsten Flagstad in Rhinemaiden plaits was making one of her umpteenth farewell performances; the second in Moscow; and the third some years ago in London.

In Russia I saw Gounod's *Faust*, the one about the doctor who was contemplating suicide just as Mephistopheles popped up in timely fashion out of a puff of hellish smoke. Personally, I didn't find it convincing because Faust, when asked what he craved most in return for his immortal soul, chose to be young again. As he was four-foot high with very fat legs, I thought this was a bit of a waste. Never mind the grey hairs, he needed inches.

The last opera was *La Bohème*, the one in which the painter treats the girl in the garret so appallingly. Which brings me to the telegram and the exhibition. Two weeks ago my son received a letter from his father, Ned, in New Zealand saying that he had experienced a mild heart attack. My son told my daughter, who promptly threw a wobbly on the grounds that she might never see her Daddy again. As it was a cleaning day – I may have mentioned my staff problems in previous articles – the head domestic and bottle-washer rang Nelson, N.Z., and during the course of an increasingly tired and emotional, not to say expensive, global telephone conversation, I apparently promised to pay half the cost of an airline ticket which would wing Dad, after an absence of sixteen years, back to the bosom of his family.

We must have been very persuasive – I blame the cleaner – because two days later the telegram arrived. It read: *Arriving mid Sept. Where am I staying? Repeat, where do I stay? Lear caper not on. Love, Ned.* The Lear reference eluded all of us for days, until the penny dropped and we remembered the King who was thrown out by his daughters and ended up, minus his marbles, exposed to the elements on the blasted Heath.

The opera I saw at Covent Garden on Saturday, to which I was taken by my friend Malcolm, was Beethoven's *Fidelio, or Married Love*. It was a splendid night, and we sat in a box, courtesy of Charles. The story, in case you're unfamiliar with it, concerns a man called Florestan who's languishing in a dungeon, and his wife who disguises herself as a fella in order to release him. I can only suppose that spectacles hadn't been invented in those days, or else belief was meant to be suspended, because a blind moggie would have sensed that there was something female about a grave-digger with a forty-inch bust.

I found it a bit near the bone. I once threw £100 in pound notes out of the kitchen window to appease someone who was threatening to wring Ned's neck. I know it's not the same: Ned was being hounded by creditors, whereas Florestan had done something politically out of order, but you can see the connection. Had I but seen *Fidelio*, I could have cried out, when scattering the readies, '*Ha! Welch ein Augenblick!*' (Ha, what a moment!) rather than 'Please go away, I feel sick.'

On her birthday I took my second daughter to see *La Bohème*. We both cried. Poor Mimi! I'm not suggesting that Ned left me with tiny frozen hands, though I do suffer from chilblains, but we did live in an attic when he painted a portrait of Bessie Braddock. When he and I were courting in those dear, dead days beyond recall we visited a beauty spot called Loggerheads, known locally as Buggerlugs. We went there twice; once in summer when I was stung by a bee, and once at Easter when our footsteps, treading side by side, left tracks in the snow. I named that place the Blue Mountains.

Which is why, when I went to the Francis Kyle Gallery on Monday to the opening of an exhibition of paintings by Philip Hughes, I recognised the landscape. I am not a traveller – unlike Hughes, who has followed the Inca Trail of Peru, flown in a helicopter above the rice fields of the new territories of Hongkong and back-packed in the Blue Mountains of Australia. I have watched his progress for ten years. First, I thought he was a bit stiff, more of an architect than a painter. Then he went to Japan. Now he's much looser, particularly in a lovely series of paintings entitled *Ski-tracks in the Snow*. Hughes is into capturing the past, and I approve of that.

Someone has got to put down, whether in words or on canvas, or in song, what the rest of us went through, what we meant, what we felt. Otherwise, the lament of Florestan, stuck in his dungeon, '*Gott, welch Dunkel hier*' (God! What darkness) might serve as an epitaph for us all.

Footnote. For Fred's eyes only: Dear Fred in Bath, You write that you were passing through London last week and happened to take home a copy of the *Standard* in which I mentioned my fear of flying, or indeed, any form of travel. I am grateful for your suggestion that I take up tap-dancing as it is something I was quite good at in my youth. I tap-danced my way into the hearts of our troops during the war as a child member of Miss Thelma Broadbent's Ensemble, Southport.

Grateful as I am for the thought, I do not think I am as yet ready for working men's clubs. I do hope the extra top hat you have purchased will not go to waste.

No, I do not know the hotel you mention, but it sounds very nice.

11. Evening in Provence

I've always had a thing about Napoleon, though I've often mixed him up with Kiss-Me-Hardy Nelson. Once, years ago, I went to Christie's, or maybe Sotheby's, where his thingie was up for auction. It was in a glass case and looked like an elongated damson. No wonder Josephine looks so morose in her portraits.

I've just come back from my holidays, having spent eleven days in a hill village in the Luberon region of the South of France. Yes, it was lovely, and sunny and, though it once threatened to rain, it never did.

I won't bore you with descriptions of the sunsets and the cheeses and the Mistral blowing gently across the surface of the swimming pool; nor will I mention the fig tree in the garden, the grapes ripening over the porch, the fields of sunflowers with their heads turned over their shoulders, the cherries hanging in clusters by the roadside, or the wildlife. Actually it's quite easy not to refer to the latter, as there isn't any. Apparently anything that scuttles or flies gets shot immediately. A very peaceful spot, one might think, an off-the-beaten-track sort of place, away from the main route of bloody history. Well, one couldn't be more wrong. There is a General living in the village who fought in the Resistance – until he retired, he went in and out by helicopter – and one night, through an interpreter, he recounted some of the goings-on in the past.

The road from Rome or the road to Rome – some of the minor details are a bit hazy owing to the amount of wine consumed during the General's dissertation – led through the region of the village. Their wagons had boxes fixed to the axles – the boxes contained pebbles and dropped one whenever the wheels had rotated a certain number of times. This was so that they could set up wine stations every fifteen miles.

Charlemagne came, and St Paul, and St Francis of Assisi, though not in a group. There were so many cannon balls whizzing around through the centuries that the locals have got used to walking with their heads down. In the sixteenth century they had a religious war and the village was in a state of siege for fifteen months. In the middle of it they held a sort of hot-pot supper night in the General's house for the garrison men and all the notable Catholics. The enemy scaled the walls – it's a bit like Masada round there – overpowered the guards and put everyone to the sword. Here the General took us through to his kitchen to point out a rusty stain on the wall. Later we went into his back garden to see the tomb of one of Napoleon's generals. He died of gout and was buried standing upright for some reason that I can't remember.

The following evening we were invited to another friend's house and told that something was going to happen of which we must not breathe a word, ever, to a living soul. All would become clear in the next half hour. We were left alone in the drawing-room, and then all the lights went out. Shortly afterwards our host appeared dressed in black, carrying a candle and looking extremely pale. There were six of us, but only Francesca was called. We stayed there in the dark for what seemed like a long time and then there was a terrible scream. Francesca's young man grew quite agitated, but we told him not to be silly. I admit it wasn't the sort of evening I'm used to " do pop round for a cup of tea and a digestive – but I was almost sure we'd get out alive. I was the fourth to go, beckoned from the doorway. I was told by my host that this was not a game, but very serious indeed. The future of both France and England depended on it. I was about to smile in a sheepish kind of way when some ladies in ball gowns and funny hats came running down the stone stairs. They were chattering away, and then they disappeared. I was told Napoleon was upstairs lying in a coffin and that I could ask him three questions. I mustn't touch him, on pain of death. I thought they'd dug up the General's general, but

I was assured it was the other one, the one who retreated from Moscow that nasty winter.

Now I've always been very keen on Bonaparte – did you see Rod Steiger in the film? – so I fairly rushed up the stairs. The attic room was enormous. A few cannon balls had chipped holes in the wall but it was otherwise sound. Boney was lying on a trestle table, bound head to foot in white cloth. I was sat right next to him, and in the candlelight I could see the outline of his noble nose.

'What's it like on the other side?' I asked, and was reprimanded because I'd forgotten he could only answer yes or no. 'Is it cold on the other side?' I amended.

He nodded.

'Do you regret things?' I said inadequately.

This time he moved his head from side to side.

'Were you poisoned?'

His reaction to this was dreadful. He let out a roar, reared up from somewhere behind me and then tried to throttle me. If I'd had a weak heart I would have been a goner. I swear there was no one else in the room apart from me and my host – and the corpse of course.

I was taken to the bathroom where Francesca and her young man were crouched in the dark. She was still shaking. We never got to the bottom of it. The supposition was that someone had been lying down the other way round. When the head appeared to nod, it was really a pair of feet. Those hands round my throat had definitely come from behind. All in all, it was a rum evening.

Did I mention that the Marquis de Sade lived over the wall? Actually, his is the next village, Lacoste, but you can see the castle from our graveyard. We always visit there for fish and chips and a game of table football in the back room – I'm referring to the local tabac, not the castle which is falling down and couldn't accommodate a chip fryer. Recently someone has given money for the stones to be stuck together again; the moat's been dug out and a temporary drawbridge is in place. Bats flit about the place at dusk, and security men patrol at night because American matrons keep rushing

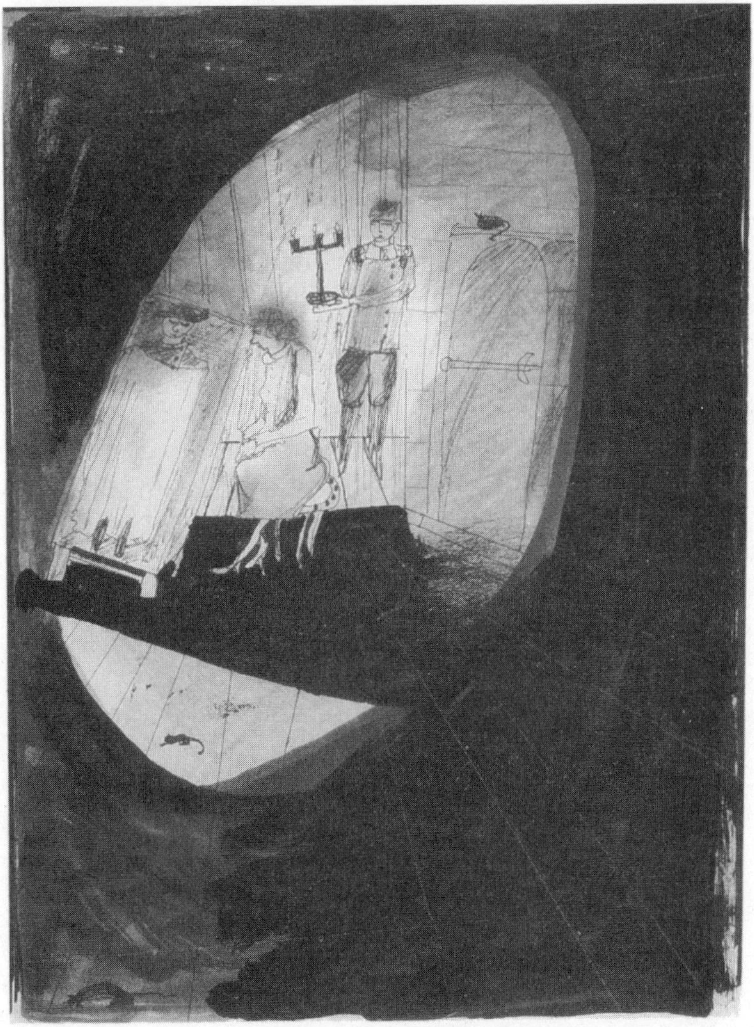

'Were you poisoned?'

about the ruins by moonlight, hoping for the atrocities to begin.

Footnote. My train was just drawing into Avignon when I went to the loo. I was sitting there when the door burst open and a lady said, 'So sorry,' and closed the door. A second later she thrust it open again and cried, 'I've read you ... you're Brenda Bainbridge.' I'm afraid I wasn't very responsive. In that position it's not easy to discuss one's novels in depth.

12. Attic nights

My youngest, who took offence at my dancing in the café at Cassiopi, is now pregnant. Not only, aged seven, did she dash the drink from my lips, she also kicked Captain Ouzo on the shins. The eminent philosopher mentioned, who died for four minutes was Freddie Ayer.

There was a very good Wogan on telly the other night, when we almost had a real discussion as to whether more channels on the box would be good for us or not. Just as Mrs Whitehouse was ticking off Andrew Neil and Ludovic Kennedy the programme ended, though not before Ludo, in response to a complaint of Mrs W's, managed to murmur: 'Nothing ever leads anywhere on television.' I could have done with another hour of it. On second thoughts, I couldn't; it would have meant missing *Brookside* and that thrilling episode in which Billy ran away to look at the river before Sheila finally got over her scruples and climbed into bed with him in the garage. I switched off after that – overcome. But television goes on all night, doesn't it? A bit of this and a bit of that; science, politics, nature study and murder. Funny how so little in these long telly nights ever makes you want to know more.

I mention this sad fact because I've been reading something called *Attic Nights* all week, or rather a book by the scholar Leofranc Holford-Strevens about the author of a book of the same title, and oddly enough *Attic Nights* was written with that express purpose in mind – I mean, to stimulate the curiosity. The author says at the beginning that he wanted merely to jot down a few nuggets of information that might amuse lively minds and so arouse further interest in a variety of subjects. Not wanting to bore the pants off the reader, and bearing in mind the dictum that much learning doesn't often make for more intelligence, he selected his subjects with care and touched on them with a light hand, giving us a little bit of law, medicine, language and philosophy and, with an admirable sense of priorities, a fair amount of sex.

I suppose it could be described as a sort of *Reader's Digest* for the upwardly mobile of the second century A.D. I haven't finished the book about the book yet – it's not what you call a quick read – but I am growing more and more curious by the page. The author of *Attic Nights*, an Italian called Aulus Gellius, lived in Athens. He had many friends and they all spent a lot of time drinking, wandering around second-hand bookshops and going to dinner parties. Once, after a storm-tossed boat ride from Cassiopi to the mainland, which by his account would afterwards have confined most of us to bed for a fortnight, Gellius rushed off into town and bought some learned dirty books (mucky that is) and read them in two days. I know Cassiopi, which is why I got so excited by the story. I dined at a café there with the children, and on the way back from ordering five portions of pig and chips was asked to dance by the village dwarf who was known as Captain Ouzo. Not wanting to hurt his feelings I cavorted for at least ten minutes, waving a handkerchief in that fashion made famous by Anthony Quinn. It was the night my youngest daughter dashed a glass of wine from my lips and said she hoped she was adopted.

Gellius' subjects range wide – covering marriage, fire prevention, the advisability of breast-feeding, the corruptive influence of too much money, the 'thin and bloodless' usage of inexact words, and the contradiction implied in the sentence ... 'he had eloquence enough but little wisdom'. One way and another, to my mind, Aulus Gellius was a life-enhancer. His best friend, a philosopher and writer from Arles, dyed his hair, wore after-shave and didn't have any testicles. Despite this, he was gay, a terrible womaniser and a drunkard to boot. He was once taken to court for adultery, which is quite something when one thinks of his disability.

Gellius says that even when legless his friend was sensitive enough not to monopolise the conversation.

I was discussing philosophy with Professor Hugh Lloyd-Jones the other day – one does that sort of thing in Camden Town – and we touched on the much-publicised experience of an eminent philosopher who recently died for four minutes, during which time he was puzzled to see a scarlet glow at the end of a tunnel. 'Not surprising,' snapped Professor Lloyd-Jones, 'every atheist who reaches the next world makes straight for the red-light district.'

All in all, I've decided to cut out watching television and read instead. I think Billy Corkhill's been doing the same thing, because before he went into the garage with Sheila he told her that he was deeper than he appeared. 'You asked me what the river meant to me,' he said, 'and I said I didn't know, because I'm not supposed to know, am I? But I do know. The river's been flowing on for hundreds of years and it'll be flowing on long after we've gone.'

Now if *that* isn't leading somewhere I don't know what is.

13. Good behaviour

I think the following is quite profound, not to say sad. It must be hell to be young.

I was asked to Derbyshire the other week to speak at a writers' residential course. To my astonishment my daughter offered to come with me. She said she was at a loose end and could always write up her memoirs. She's been writing her memoirs for two years now, ever since she was 20. Before we went we made a pact; she promised not to start laughing as soon as I opened my mouth if I promised not to follow her about with an ashtray or turn down offers of alcoholic refreshment on her behalf. She said that if anyone asked her what she did for a living she was going to say she was a tree surgeon, and a good part of the journey was taken up trying to identify various elms and oaks. Halfway there she gave up on the idea and switched to being a veterinary student.

As we drove up to the house we passed a herd of cows and she said she wasn't going to pretend to be a vet after all because a cow might fall ill and what would she do if she was asked to save it? I was a little more agitated at this than I might have been if I hadn't remembered that holiday in Scotland when she told everyone that I'd had her committed at twelve for persistent shop-lifting. As it happened she behaved beautifully, except for telling Mr Matthews that she couldn't take her hat off because she had ringworm. And then I noticed during supper that she was looking rather desperate, even sad, as opposed to sulky. When later I asked her what the matter was she said she'd never been with so many old people in all her life, and wasn't it awful – everyone half-deaf or half-blind or half-crippled. She was exaggerating of course. Most people were the same age as me, on that middle ground between spectacles for reading and spectacles for everything, and those few genuinely elderly persons among us were notable more for their mental agility than their physical infirmities.

I told her not to be ridiculous, not to be rude; I came out with all the platitudes usual on such occasions. It was only afterwards that I understood what had so outraged her. It was not, as I had first thought, that she shrank from the reflection of her own mortality, simply that she was not accustomed to conversing with anybody over the age of twenty-five. She has no grandparents, no uncles, and communication with friends of mine is generally restricted to a nod or at most a request for a cigarette. It's not that she's against us, as she points out – more that we fade into the background and seem part of the furniture.

I see her dilemma – she was not brought up to be a mixer. In my day we belonged to our parents and accompanied them everywhere: to church, to the shops, on those endless high-tea visits (half a tomato, a slice of spam and a lettuce leaf) to the few blood relations and the many aunts and uncles who were no relation at all.

We had to sit up straight and remember F.H.B. (family hold back) and only accept a second piece of damp seed cake when it would positively choke us. We had to talk about what we intended to do when we left school, and what our best subjects were. On the return visits, even if we had anything so outlandish as a room of our own, it would have been tantamount to spitting on the carpet to announce that we were going up to it, unless it was to fetch our handkerchiefs or our scrapbooks.

And we were expected to sing for our suppers. I was regularly called upon to recite 'The Slave's Dream', which I had foolishly boasted of knowing by heart. We were part of the furniture with a vengeance, precious ornaments perpetually on display. Mother's girls and boys, every one of us. I often wonder what they would have found to talk about, those adults of the past, if they hadn't been permanently engaged in putting us through the third degree. I even had an 'auntie' who inquired about my bowels, though this may have been kindly meant, as I was rather stocky.

Before we left Derbyshire the news came through of the mass-shootings in Hungerford. We were all shaken, including my daughter, but travelling back on the train she refused to read the newspapers. I kept oohing and aahing and reading out bits to her, and finally she told me to be quiet. She said she wasn't interested in the sensational details. Didn't I know it was happening all the time? But that's America, I protested, and she said, rubbish, it was happening all over the world, it always had. Why, 'my lot' were always going on about the First World War or the second one, getting misty-eyed over Dunkirk or pinning paper poppies to our lapels in memory of the Somme. And we had jumped up and down with glee over the Falklands. I said that was different, and she said it wasn't, it was exactly the same thing, people being violently killed.

'You can't expect our lot to spot the difference,' she said.

Footnote. I was ticked off badly last week by Mr L of no fixed address who said I 'betrayed my ignorance when I admitted going to the loo when the train was standing in the station'. But I never said it was standing; I wrote that it was arriving, meaning still rolling along the tracks. And does he mean ignorant of the rules or – as I suspect – badly brought up? I do assure him that there are two Commandments which I've tried very hard never to break: the one about the train, and thou shalt not eat a shop-bought meat pie.

14. Principles of action

Nothing hidden here, simply a blow-by-blow account of tram-lines and a wander through a churchyard.

History, it has been said, is philosophy teaching by examples. If I were asked for a precise definition of this piece of wisdom I'd be all of a dither, but if an inexact explanation was called for I would confidently state that it has something to do with song contests and my Auntie Nellie. Perhaps I should elaborate. Last week I visited both Liverpool and the Lake District. In Liverpool I watched some of the making of a film adapted by John McGrath from a novel I wrote called *The Dressmaker*. It's about my Auntie Margo, my Auntie Nellie and my Dad, and it's set during the war when the Yanks were over here, overpaid and oversexed.

My Auntie Nellie, whom I may have mentioned before in this column – she's the one lying desiccated inside an urn in Anfield cemetery – was a great respecter of furniture. During the Blitz she shoved all the tables and chairs into the boxroom so that they wouldn't get dusty. She said that in wartime people got lax attitudes, towards furniture in particular, and she waged her own fierce little war of preservation. The story ends in tears, of course, with Auntie Nellie using the pinking scissors against the enemy. It's a funny experience – peculiar, not ha-ha – seeing your own past enacted on film. Joan Plowright plays Nellie and Billie Whitelaw Auntie Margo. They even look like them.

There I was in Bold Street, watching Jim O'Brien structuring a scene outside a dance hall where Wesley, the GI, attempts to knee-tremble Rita, the heroine, in a shop doorway. I was standing between Ronnie Shedlo, the producer, and an elderly lady who seemed to know a lot about film-making.

'That will cost an arm and a leg,' she said, as a tram trundled out of Slater Street and an army of extras, driving jeeps and smoking cigars, surged along the highway. I was reminded of the time, some years ago, when a television play of mine was being shot in my street in London. In the middle of a scene where Rosemary Leach and Michael Gambon were cavorting over the privet hedge, my friend Pauline came out of her house to use the phone box on the corner. She was asked if she'd mind waiting a second. She said she bloody well would. Later – a year or so later when we were again on speaking terms (after all, it *was* my TV play she'd brought to a standstill) – I told her that the three-minute telephone call to her mother in Wembley had cost £700. She said she was glad to hear it.

Anyway, after Liverpool I got on the train to the Lake District to help judge a song contest in Kendal. It was jolly interesting. The winner, Brian McNeill, sang a song called 'The Devil's Only Daughter'. I thought it was a bit rude, all about a man who'd been unfaithful to someone:

So though you're auld and battered, sit ye down upon my knee,
And we'll hae another glass before we go.
Put yer head upon my shoulder, lay yer back upon my breast,
And hae patience while I rosin up my bow.

I identified with the poor girl immediately and it was only during a discussion in the judges' room that I learnt that the subject was a fiddle, not a woman. How was I to know?

However, it's what happened afterwards that ties up with my opening paragraph. I was driven by Jennifer to Flookburgh, which is up a bit from Kendal and past Grange-over-Sands. Though neither a pretty village nor a place of historical interest, Flookburgh is none the less part of life's rich pattern, if only of mine, for it was here that John, having arrived from Scotland, was recorded in the parish register as being the father of William, born 1846, who was the father of

Dick, born 1889, who was my Dad. I can't say we found anybody of my name mouldering in Cartmel churchyard, or in Corpse Lane for that matter, though I did teeter across the marshy ground in my two-tone high-heeled shoes, specs on, hand outstretched to tear away the moss and the clinging ivy. I suspect my lot were too poor to afford a headstone.

I was very conscious in the Lake District of that article in one of the Sunday supplements about the comparative values of property across the North/South divide: you know, that business about a one-bedroom flat in Kentish Town being worth a castle in Wigan with an outside loo set in 9,000 acres. I kept adding up for Jennifer's benefit how much that tree, that wall, that outhouse would cost in NW1. When she told me how much they would actually cost in Cumbria I felt a bit like Lenny in *Mice and Men,* and only lack of drink kept me from begging her to tell me about the rabbits. Which brings me back to that first paragraph, which refers to the study of the principles of human action or conduct. A principle, as we all know, is to do with that from which something originates, an ultimate basis, a primary element which determines particular results.

In other words it's a fundamental source, as in Flookburgh or my Auntie Nellie.

Footnote. My grandma on the maternal side, nothing to do with Flookburgh, swore by a magazine called *Red Letter*. It was so sizzling she used to hide it behind the dolly tub in the back yard. A kind reader has just sent me a cutting from a similar publication called *Building Design,* dated June 12, which lists unlikely 'liaisons' between architects and 'media women'. Among others, Anna Ford is linked with Richard Reid, Peter Moro with that marvellous novelist Marghanita Laski, Sue Arnold with L. Apicella and me with Patrick Hodgkinson. I don't think they're that unlikely. I have nothing but praise for Mr Hodgkinson who understood my predicament when we travelled in a propeller-driven aeroplane above Scapa Flow. I hate flying and he hates heights. Both of us held on to our principles.

15. Forty years on

My brother died a month afterwards. He was at his desk in his solicitor's office and he cried out, 'Help me', and, because he had a reputation as a practical joker, nobody took any notice. Twenty-four hours later, felled by a massive stroke, he died.

We all know how our children alter things that happened in the past, how they harp on the time we disgraced them by crying into our handkerchiefs at the primary school Nativity play, when the truth was that we had a bad cold; or the occasion they brought home a little friend for tea and found us prostrate on the living-room floor in a stupor of migraine; which they've referred to ever since as a stupor of quite another sort. Only last year I was accused of playing rounders in the Park in my knickers and vest, and when I was stumped out I apparently ran up a tree and refused to come down. How the young distort the truth! I bring this up because a few days ago I returned to a village that I last visited forty-odd years ago.

I'm not going to reveal where it is because I don't want to upset the residents. Suffice it to say that it's up North, in the country, and that my maternal grandfather, Jack James Baines, first went there in the twenties to manage a barytes mine (which is a mineral they used to crush and put into paint to make it stick to the wall – it looks a bit like a lump of rock sprinkled with star dust and if it gets into cow's hooves you have to kill the cow). Mr Baines brought my mother to the village as a child – she once told me she went down the mine with a searchlight attached to her helmet (silly girl, it could only have been a candle) – and later she took my brother and me there for holidays. I first remember going there in about 1942. I know it was then because I went

Mad for land girls.

to an army camp and I won a prize for the girl with the biggest eyes. It could have been ears, I suppose.

The village had one pub, which took in paying guests, a dozen cottages, a church, a workhouse and two or three manor houses. Rural England at its best, you might say, just so long as one only stayed there for three weeks of the year. There was a stuffed stoat on the windowsill of the snug bar in the pub. Its belly, oozing straw, had laid a granite egg.

'Whatever happened to the stoat?' I asked my brother, who now lives three miles away, 'the one that had laid an egg?'

'Don't talk soft,' he said. 'It was a stone. Stoats don't lay eggs.'

Now, I know in my head as well as the next man that a stoat is a mammal, but until that moment I hadn't realised that that particular stoat was incapable of laying an egg. Thinking about it, it isn't normal, let alone possible, for a stoat to have a Caesarian birth, but then you could say – in those secretive days – that it wasn't normal for me to be molested by the cowman who lodged in the attic of the pub beneath the sides of bacon, crusted all over with salt, from which the maggots were brushed when the breakfast rashers were sliced.

I didn't think my brother was in a receptive mood to discuss the cowman, so I didn't mention him, but I brought up the honeymoon couples who had come to the village in our childhood. In those days the forty-eight-hour wedding pass was prevalent and it was mostly the RAF who came to the pub. We children were told to leave the young couple alone. When the bridegroom aviator left, the bride stayed on, sitting on the bench outside the front door, watching the skies for that one Spitfire that mattered. My brother said he didn't remember any of that. Actually, his words were: 'You've got a blooming active imagination.'

There was a lot of emotion in those days, slopping about the fields and the haylofts. The land-girls created havoc. There was something about their cello-shaped corduroy breeches that aroused lust. Mostly they provoked that innocent, more dangerous type of longing labelled 'love', but once or twice passion raged. I overheard the gossip while crouched in the privy shed behind the bowling green, reading my *Girl's Crystal* magazine, the sunlight running like glass beads along the cracks of the wooden roof.

When I returned to the village last week and spoke to elderly inhabitants, I expected mysteries to be solved.

'That chap,' I asked, 'who went berserk with his rabbit gun on account of the land-girl from Somerset? And Y, who fell into a decline, watered the beer and put his hook through his lower lip while casting a salmon down by the river? And what about Z, who was overfond of that evacuee up at the Hall?'

I didn't get very far. For a moment I thought I detected a sparkle in the collective eye, but it was gone in an instant.

'There weren't any salmon in the river,' said one. 'We didn't have no evacuees up at the Hall,' said another.

So much for memories. Perhaps the past can never be seen as a whole and is always a few crumbling fragments picked up from the ruins of a once-solid present – everything else is as dead as the dodo, as extinct as the egg-laying stoat.

Footnote. Dear Mrs L of NW6, It was very kind of you to defend me at your local pub, and in such a spirited way. I really don't know what to suggest about your particular 'cross'. You are obviously a sympathetic person, albeit under a strain, and I think you would live to regret putting something in the food. Could you not get comfort from that old adage about every cloud having a silver lining? Cliché it may be, but I have found it to be true on many occasions. Yes, I suppose I did have something of a sad early life, and, as you rightly observe, such experiences 'scar one', but I do assure you I am perfectly cheerful now.

16. Waiting for Papa

I'm not going to enlarge on the events recounted here: they are too painful. The moment he set eyes on me my ex said I looked very withered. The last night he was here the cleaner confronted him. How could he have walked out on his children all those years ago? His response was pretty predictable, given the guilt we all feel. He said, 'This is all very boring', and caught a taxi to the airport.

I got the feeling last week that the Fates were definitely against my children seeing their long-lost Papa ever again. I had ordered the car to take us to the airport, swept the hall carpet for the umpteenth time, stocked up the fridge, bought the cat a new flea collar and generally done all those things which are usually left undone, but I had a niggling feeling that I was whistling in the wind. And that was before the storm.

The day before I had taken part in an arts programme which required me to visit the Seven Dwarfs in a grotto in Hamley's toy shop. I crouched on a little chair inside a little house and Doc and Grumpy kept thumping each other with very little hammers. There was no sign of the wicked witch but she'd obviously called because that dreaded apple, red as sin and twice as deadly, was rolling about in the middle of the table. Snow White was sitting outside on a grassy knoll, a bluebird perched on her finger, holding court to a circle of mechanical bunny rabbits. No, Hamley's aren't trying to remind us of how many shopping days are left to Christmas, just joining in the celebrations to mark the 50th anniversary of the first showing of Walt Disney's classic animated feature.

Later that day I went to see a preview of the film and for all of twenty seconds watched appalled as Snow White fluttered her eyelashes, simpered and generally behaved like a cross between Zsa Zsa Gabor and Dame Edna Everage. Then I was hooked. So what, if she seemed to want nothing more than to dust and cook for those diminutive men until her Prince arrived to carry her off? What did it matter that during the past fifty years we have been trying to free ourselves from just such a sentimental, fettered image of womanhood? Who gives a fig for feminism, for emancipation, faced with that glorious innocent girl with the tip-tilted nose and the rosebud mouth who gets through the housework with a song in her heart and a flock of bluebirds to help out with the washing up. In spite of everything, it seems to me that every boy still sees himself as that Prince on the white charger and every girl is still content to wait for him.

I went with Brendan, my secretary, who's only a young lad. He was supposed to be taking notes but he kept sniffing and wiping his eyes. He admitted to crying – well, to having watery eyes. He thought it had something to do with childhood, to his having seen the film when small; he said it may have triggered off other memories that he'd mislaid or buried. He wasn't about to say what they were because he was too busy blowing his nose, but I knew what he meant.

I had forgotten that Snow White went off at the end without the Dwarfs. It quite upset me. I was sure I remembered her refusing to leave without them. Brendan said my mother had probably told me that to stop me howling; it was obvious that they had to stay behind on account of the diamond mine and the country's economy.

Anyway, I was still a bit weepy the next day when we set off for the airport to meet my ex-husband who was arriving from New Zealand after an absence of fifteen years. It didn't help that the storm had carried off the rambling rose from the front garden, or that a branch or two of the tree next door had landed across the hedge and flattened it, any more than it was encouraging to be driven along with a man on the wireless informing us that the runway was closed and that we should turn back if we valued our lives.

I was all for doing as I was told, but my son had never been behind the wheel of a Jaguar before and was damned if he was going to be done out of the experience. It wasn't as if he had his eyes on the road either; he was too busy trying to ring up his girlfriend on the car telephone. My daughter, in the back with Charlie and Darling Bertie, was having a miserable time. Charlie had found all the remote control knobs and the windows were whizzing up and down and the seats kept shooting backwards and forwards. Once I was nearly ejected through the roof. The children thought they wouldn't recognise Dad; my son thought he'd probably be in a wheelchair or possibly bald. When he did come through customs he appeared thinner and his beard was speckled, but he was pretty fit. For ten minutes I thought he had changed, and after that he looked exactly as I remembered him.

On the way back to Camden Town there were terrible traffic jams. We were stationary for hours. The grandchildren were hungry and wanted apples. Grandad hopped out to find the nearest greengrocers, and at that moment the traffic started moving again. We lost him for ages. My son said it was funny the old man coming all that way and then disappearing without trace.

It's strange how people mellow with age. We haven't had a cross word since he arrived, and he's out there now with his little hammer mending the fence. For my part, I'm doing quite a bit of dusting though as yet I haven't felt compelled to burst into song.

Footnote. Some time ago I received a very nice letter from Ms Rhoda Comstock telling me about a novel she had written entitled 'As Flies to Wanton Boys'. Following my article about the Booker Prize, she has written again and kindly invited me to present the Cooker Prize for Fiction at East Clyst. The prize, a New World cooker donated by Canon Trewit, is apparently to be shared between two authors. Quite how they are going to divide the cooker remains to be seen, but I do congratulate everyone concerned on their enterprise.

17. Not the same

Christmas is always hell, particularly for whoever is claiming to be the head of the family. All that wasted money, all that festive merriment torpedoed by the telly.

I listened to a discussion on television last week about the philosopher David Hume. Both the interviewer and the expert were dazzling in their command of language, and neither appeared to need to draw breath between sentences. It was the sort of lovely chat that made one's brain hurt, and I was so taken by the performance and excited by the content that I fetched a piece of paper and attempted to write down what was said. At the time it made perfect sense but half an hour later it had gone in one ear and whizzed out the other, which was disappointing because I'd had high hopes of astonishing people over supper with my riveting conversation.

Reading my scribbled notes, I deciphered these sentences: 'We see them today, we see them tomorrow, but give them a bag and they are not the same people' and 'We can't totally prove that the sun will rise tomorrow any more than we can prove that it will soon be Christmas.' The last word was heavily underlined and there was a doodle in the margin of an anorexic robin. It's obvious that the first part of the sentence is very profound, but what of the second? Is it possible that old Hume was into Christmas in a big way, or did my attention wander, causing me unconsciously to substitute one word for another, therefore expressing a deeply buried anxiety concerning the coming festive season. Whatever it was, better out than in, as they say, and, as a burden shared is considered to be a burden halved, I hasten to worry the life out of the rest of you.

What *are* we going to do for Christmas? Is it to be the same old ritual round the rickety table in the front room? Or could this be the year for innovations? Hotels are obviously not a good thing. Quite apart from the expense I doubt if any of my family would be allowed into the dining-room in the sort of clothing they habitually wear. Other people's houses are definitely out. When one's children touchingly insist that they prefer Christmas at home, we all know what they really mean – the right to fall asleep either across or under the table. Having been to the pub the night before, they are far too frail to do anything more strenuous than lift up a jar of pickled onions, let alone pass it round or be helpfully polite.

Numbers are important. Far better to have a room full of bad-tempered and inebriated guests than the average family sitting round the best table-cloth wearing paper hats and yawning. I used to think it would be nice for the children to have an old person present, a really old one with an ear trumpet or something endearing like that, but we could never find one. My own mother wouldn't come to me for Christmas, preferring to go to my brother's house. She said I didn't have the equipment, which was unfair as my neighbour Pauline used to lend knives and forks, at least until the misunderstanding over the stair carpet. I've not forgotten the mortification of applying to the Council for an old person – they had a sort of rent-a-senior-citizen scheme – and being turned down.

Apparently Council elderly are very fussy and stipulate all sorts of conditions, including floor-covering. I lent my carpeting to Pauline the year *her* mother came for Christmas, and she wouldn't return it. She said it was a death trap, anyway, and that she was doing me a favour hanging on to it.

So what about renting a cottage, a large one in a bleak and desolate place? In theory, this idea has gone down very well with my lot. Down with all that food: a tin or two of sardines will do and the money saved can be spent on extra liquid refreshment. Long walks are talked about, open fires, wassailing in the woods. We might even find some old person in the snow – possibly trapped in a rabbit snare – who could

Fetching an old person for Christmas.

be forcibly brought back to share a sardine and enliven us with stories of the good old days when a threepenny bit and an orange in an old sock spelled happiness. Why, with a threepenny bit one could buy a plum tart at the baker's and still have enough money for a holiday for eight in Blackpool.

My youngest daughter got quite carried away at the thought of such a Christmas, insisting that we should disconnect any television set that might be there and entertain each other instead. And we mustn't buy expensive presents, not even for the grandchildren. We should economise and make things out of twists of paper and bits of wool. She herself would play tunes on the cello. As she hasn't a cello it seemed possible she was thinking of improvising one out of those bits of wool previously mentioned; but no, she wants me to buy her a proper one for Christmas. So much for economy. Seances have been mentioned, and sing-songs, and that story about the monkey's paw in which the three wishes bring such misery.

Anyway, I'm thinking about a cottage. There's plenty of time, isn't there, between now and Christmas? I've already started putting twists of paper into an old carrier bag. Every time it crosses my mind that it's a waste of time I remember that mysterious comment of Hume's: 'We see them today, we see them tomorrow, but give them a bag and they are not the same people.' Quite so! It's making more sense by the minute.

Footnote. Rhoda Comstock (my correspondent of the past two weeks) has sent me an alarming note to do with the Cooker Prize for Fiction. Apparently someone called Reg was responsible for installing the cooker for the lucky winner, and blew up two cottages in East Clyst. Fortunately there was no loss of life, but the owners were none too pleased. One should always beware of amateurs.

18. Weaker sex

We don't need more than one room to live in, it always seems to me. Not at the end. It's the furniture that requires the space. In my beginning I slept with my Mum; my dead brother – alive at the time – slept with my Dad. These nocturnal arrangements, I now realise, were an elaborate form of birth control. Also, my parents loved, rather than liked, each other. It turned them into the walking wounded.

There's a lot of impending homelessness about among my acquaintance at the moment. Every conversation seems to end with someone telling me everything would be all right if only they had a refuge to go to, a place they could call their own. George, who's been living in a recognised squat, has been given notice to quit and he swears he can't find another room for less than £60 per week. Myra wants to get away from her mother; she says she'll be had up for matricide if she's forced to live with her much longer. They have arguments about the tea-bags and her mum leaves little notes telling her how many sheets of lavatory paper should be used per calendar month. And, only yesterday, Jean, who took redundancy a year ago and departed for the Costa Del Sol, vowing never to set foot again on this isle of wind and rain, was on the phone in tears announcing her imminent return. Her fella has left her and she couldn't bear to stay in a place which holds so many memories. It's sad really. When I last saw her she was whirling round the floor of a taverna shaking a tambourine and shouting 'Olé' with the best of them.

It all makes me very uneasy because I'm aware that I have a spare room, if not two, and I'm thinking of buying a gramophone record of John Gielgud reciting that speech about someone or other being drowned in a Malmsey butt.

I remember it from many years ago; there's a lot of clanking and wailing – I think it's about the two princes being smothered in the Tower – and a dog barking in the background. I could put it on whenever the next homeless person calls round, just to prove that the house is fully occupied.

All this business of different places for eating in and sleeping in and entertaining is very silly. The older I get the more foolish the practice seems, not to say immoral. I get the feeling the furniture needs the house more than I do. I can see that with children, in the best of all possible worlds, a bit more space is needed, but once they've flown the nest a compatible couple could well dwell comfortably in a more restricted area. I have many happy memories of bed-sitters; there was one in Abercrombie Square, Liverpool, in which I lived, briefly, when I was fifteen. It was so big and dark that it resembled one of those gloomy sets in epic films of life in a tent the evening before a battle – Peter O'Toole about to scale Masada, Rod Steiger plotting to take Moscow. I was so scared I sat up all night in an armchair by the gas-fire. After three days my dad came, told the landlady I was under age, threatened her with the police and dragged me home by the ear. I was very relieved.

Then I rented a room in South Kensington. My landlady had never heard of the word privacy. She came in at all hours and dusted round me. One evening she found a man there and promptly turfed me out. I spent the night in a shop doorway with my belongings housed in carrier bags. I can't remember what happened to the man. The best bed-sit of all was in Hampstead. The boy in the room next door was studying to be a lawyer and he used to lend me his porridge pan to make soup when I came home from being an usherette.

One night I forgot to return it and, creeping in at dawn to retrieve it, he was spotted by the landlady and promptly given notice to quit. I pretended to be asleep, an innocent bystander, albeit a lying-down one.

'How dare you enter a young girl's room,' the landlady hissed. 'Think of the shock.'

'I've lost my refuge,' he wailed, as he trailed out into the street minus his porridge pan, his boxing gloves and his rugger boots strung about his innocent neck.

All of which reminds me of that series *The Refuge* on television in which a group of women hole up in a flat vowing never to let men set foot over the threshold. It has a sit-com format but upmarket dialogue, and its opposite number, in that the opposite sex is always patronised, is exemplified in any one of those male-oriented sentimental series concerning lovable hen-pecked men subjected to hysterical spouses. It's a dangerous idea for a series. A man's encounter with a prostitute or his bashful admission that he has put someone in the pudding club is often the stuff of high comedy. Reverse the roles, feature the lady of the night and the pregnant girl and one half of the population, far from finding it funny, will fall apart with guilt and howl that it's offensive. When will men acknowledge – I'm not so simple as to be unaware that they already know it – that they are the weaker sex?

Footnote. I received a lovely letter the other day from a Mr Arnold of Cold Ash, Newbury. I am far too modest to repeat the nice things he said about me; sufficient to put down some of his letter and his poem:

He chanced to meet a fairy,
  Whose clothes were very wet,
And when he saw the fairy,
  He wished they had not met.

It is rather like that, writes Mr Arnold, when I see one of your articles – if I read your words I feel like writing to say what a pleasure it is to read them – and that is inconvenient. God bless you, Mr Arnold. I do hope you're not homeless.

19. Red neckties

Not everybody mucked about with coconuts and featured on Children's Hour. I can't help feeling it's sort of historic.

I was revolting from a very early age and more than once thought of taking over a radio station and starting a rebellion. I can still remember the opening sentence of my call to arms: 'Rise up, rise up, the moment is at hand,' declaiming it on my way to school under the arch of the railway bridge, which place, being a sort of tunnel, gave it added resonance and a definite echo.

At this distance I can't remember what particular cause underlined the necessity for an uprising, but I do know that I had been reading *Red Eagle* by Dennis Wheatley, and that I carried in my satchel a picture of Marshal Budenny, a frightfully rakish-looking military man who sported the sort of moustache that drops out of a Christmas cracker and who endeared himself to his troops by addressing them as 'lousy bloodsuckers'. The point is that my fantasy was not as outlandish as it seems, for at the age of twelve I was employed by the British Broadcasting Corporation and had the run of their warren of a building in Piccadilly, Manchester.

I spent many an afternoon opening forbidden doors; catching sight of Charles Groves in dickie bow tie conducting the BBC Orchestra; eavesdropping on lonely individuals seated at green baize tables, rambling on about the mating rituals of foxes; tip-toeing into empty studios where the red light still glowed in indication of air-waves still open. I might have incited the masses to revolt if only I had gone to the local library and taken out *The Amateur's Guide to the Mysteries of the Wireless.* Far from finding such things dull I have always thought batteries, light switches, magnetic coils and U-bend plumbing to be the stuff that dreams are made of;

but alas, I lack consistency of purpose. I never mastered the wireless, but I was trained to jiggle the halves of a coconut together to reproduce the sound of an approaching horse, high-spirited or otherwise. I can also do a whinny, if I have a comb and a bit of tissue-paper handy. Such skills, extremely useful in everyday life, were taught me at the BBC in Manchester, where I was sent by my mother in response to an advertisement in the *Liverpool Echo* asking for young broadcasters for *Children's Hour*. I was not alone. Billie Whitelaw was there, Sandra and Judith Chalmers. Brian Trueman and Tony Warren, that little lad with the big ears who thought up *Coronation Street*. We were all under the supervision of Uncle Herbert, Uncle Trevor and Auntie Nan MacDonald.

Auntie Nan was headgirl; she had a huge nappy pin in her plaid skirt and she made us talk posh. I'd give a few quid to hear a recording of myself in a series called *What Will John or Janet Do?* in which I juggled my coconuts and shouted at intervals; 'Whoa up, Neddy. Hey up, Neddy' in my best Liverpool accent.

Griselda Hervey, an actress who married a Lord, and Fred Fairclough – not to be confused with Len in *Coronation Street* – and the silent screen actor Henry Ainlee played our mums and dads. Fred wore a red cravat and cavalry-twill trousers. Griselda rehearsed in a hat with a feather in it and wore a silver-fox cape slung about her shoulders. If Fred fluffed his lines he'd work his false teeth up and down in a passion and shout: 'Gawd Almighty.' Auntie Nan, glaring at him, would tap her pencil on her script until he murmured: 'Sorry infants, slip of the impure tongue.'

It was a very bohemian atmosphere; Fred wasn't the only one who sported a red neckpiece. In those days it was taken for granted that anyone who acted, wrote, played an instrument or carried a book under one arm, let alone worked for the BBC, was a socialist. It stood to reason. The higher one rose, of course, both in age and position, the more right-wing and dictatorial one was apt to become, which was an entirely satisfactory arrangement.

I'm reminded of those days in Manchester because I have just read *Truth Betrayed* by Bill West, a splendid account of the skulduggery that went on at the Beeb during the lead-up to the last war. Judging by some of the material it's not at all surprising that the BBC with Lord Reith as its Director General was regarded by the rest of Europe as a Government department. I had no idea that Guy Burgess was a BBC producer or that there were so many other spies being employed on talks programmes. Stirring stuff, and I've been racking my brains to remember whether I could have taken part in anything subversive.

Thinking about it, *Children's Hour* was a perfect vehicle for propaganda. All those very slow walks with Nomad rabbiting on about bird calls and the cry of the vixen! Perhaps he was talking in code. And what of *Toytown* in which Ernest, the policeman, was always portrayed as having lost his marbles, not to mention Dennis, the dachshund?

I understand they're bringing it back – *Children's Hour,* that is. Of course, it will have to come on at a reasonable time; I can't imagine today's little darlings being wished goodnight at twenty to six of an evening.

Footnote. Bill West went on to write a very good paperback about the dissolution of our libraries called *The Strange Rise of Semi-literate England.*

20. In concert

My idea of a good piece of music is to wake up after the closing bars and find that the bar is still open.

Why are we all so increasingly nasty to each other, I ask myself? Is it additives in the food, the fall-out from Chernobyl or simply that we no longer believe in retribution?

The other night I went to a Promenade concert, my first ever, to hear the Israel Philharmonic Orchestra, conducted by Zubin Mehta, perform some of Bruckner's Symphony No 8 in C minor. I say 'some' because Philip and I arrived late owing to a traffic jam which stretched from Baker Street to the Albert Hall. We parked the car in the middle of Hyde Park and ran a three-minute quarter of a mile to the box office but were thirty seconds too late. So were two hundred others. Lots of people wanted to go to the lavatory but were blocked by the guards on the stairway. I could have done with a spot of open heart surgery – galloping along the park without a horse and smoking at the same time is not fun – but there weren't any medical staff.

After fifteen minutes a voice over the tannoy announced that we should go to our life-boat stations. There would be a break between the *allegro moderato* and the *scherzo* during which we would be admitted. Dutifully we clustered round our respective hatches and waited. The lady at our checkpoint was a bit like Joyce Grenfell, though without a musical background and possibly deaf into the bargain because presently a man at the head of the queue danced up and down and said the *allegro moderato* had just finished.

'I am acquainted with the score,' he said. 'I demand admittance.'

'I am listening on my intercom,' retorted Joyce. 'I have not yet received the go-ahead. Anyway, they're still playing.'

At this we all looked suitably chastened; for indeed we could hear lots of violins going *scherzo* and nobody wanted to be the first to trample Joyce underfoot. We stood there listening to the second movement on the tannoy until our Leader, who obviously knew his Bruckner from his elbow, shouted that we had missed our chance. 'Take me to your manager,' he cried.

A small group of us rampaged about the foyer – that old chestnut about music soothing the savage breast is an obvious lie – until we were confronted by some very elderly gentlemen in pin-striped suits who told the mob, more or less, to shut up.

A second demand for the manager was turned down flat. 'He's a busy man,' said a geriatric usher, 'he's got more important things to attend to. Besides, we're only casual.' This last piece of information was undoubtedly true.

At that moment a youngish managerial sort of lady appeared on the scene and told Philip, who was only mildly frothing at the mouth, to pull himself together. Stung, he said he'd paid good money to hear this concert. He was told he should have got there on time, at which he pointed a trembling finger in the direction of the traffic-filled street and asked if she realised the impossibility of getting from A to Z on this particular evening.

Then he was treated to a little homily on punctuality. 'I myself,' the lady said, 'am subject to the vagaries of the rush hour' – she wore a white blouse and a very cross expression – 'but I am never late.'

'Bloody good for you,' responded Philip, by now a shade puce in the face.

The lady threw a wobbler: 'You swore at me, you swine,' she wailed. 'I'll fetch the manager.'

Well, we'd been trying to unearth him since half way through the *allegro moderato* bit, but just as she rushed off the door into the auditorium was miraculously unbolted and we entered the concert hall as the third movement was beginning: *Feierlich langsam: doch nicht schleppend* (solemn and slow, but not dragging). I had been caught with a ciggie in my mouth and lots of people waved their hands about, either conducting or protesting at the tobacco smoke.

It was a marvellous concert. I think one can tell when something is good even if one doesn't know an E flat from a B minor, and it was very loud, which I always find uplifting. Unfortunately there was no piano. Do you remember that film about Liszt with Dirk Bogarde playing the lead? It was memorable for the scene in which some ladies started chatting in the middle of a recital and all the extras cried out, 'Psst for Liszt.'

In the middle of a particularly loud bit I found myself daydreaming I was sitting in the front row of the Liverpool Philharmonic Hall the night my carbuncle burst. I can't remember what piece was being played, but the eruption on the side of my nose was throbbing in time to the music. After ten minutes or so of excruciating agony, and just as the cymbals clashed, the carbuncle exploded. I was amazed my head hadn't flown off. I asked my companion for a handkerchief. He said, without looking at me, 'Yes, it is moving, isn't it?' and lent me his scarf.

After the present concert we went to a fish-and-chip shop with a composer called Nick Cole who knew all about Bruckner. Apparently he was shy, religious, obsessed by numbers, sexually excited by very young girls, a genius but not very bright. When his seventh symphony was first played he was so chuffed by the performance that he pressed a shilling into the conductor's hand and told him to buy himself a drink. Oh yes, and he liked going to the local morgue to look at bodies.

Philip said the row in the foyer had put him off the concert. He hadn't been able to concentrate. Just one word of apology, one small expression of regret would have made a world of difference. We all agreed that such an admission of involvement was a lot to expect these days. I think it's a virus, this lack of courtesy, and it's spreading, like measles or AIDS, *nicht schleppend doch mit Hast* (not dragging, but fast). I reckon one in four of us is infected.

Footnote. Last week I received the following letter from foreign parts: Dear Sir, First, excuse me make bold to bother you, because we never know each other. I have gone to trouble to get your helping. I am a Chinese young man making a new style swimsuit for women. I intend to apply to be patient. So I seek advice from you and helping in my task. I find your address from a material and know you have written a *Dressmaker*. Please send money for getting patients. This swimsuit will go down heavenly. Excuse me, Best Regards, Zhang Li-Yong.

21. Christmas ghost

I keep wondering whether the abrupt departure of Miss Smith has left permanent scars on the minds of those little ones in her care. Have they perhaps, in adult life, behaved oddly on hearing the opening bars of The Grand Old Duke of York, rather like that unfortunate man in The Manchurian Candidate?

Something happened yesterday; I had a sudden urge to learn to play the piano, and I saw a ghost. The ghost sighting came after the urge and in broad daylight. It was downright spooky, though hardly frightening. Let me set the scene.

I had just returned from the BBC in Portland Place and was standing looking out of the back window of my laboratory at the top of the house. On the way home my cab had stopped at some traffic lights and I distinctly heard through the wound-down window – I was smoking, you see, so I had to put up with the fresh air – the sound of a piano playing something difficult, one of those pieces full of F sharps and B minors. Immediately I made up my mind to take it up – the piano, that is. I would start with less classical stuff – 'Roses of Picardy' for instance – and work my way upwards. Anyway, there I was in the laboratory mentally flexing my fingers when I saw the ghost. I may have pointed out that the 'laboratory' is where I keep my word-processor, an instrument which the cleaner thinks of as a fiendish crucible of language, hence the posh name. The view from the window, now that it is winter, is somewhat bleak – the backs of houses, a few stripped trees, various clumps of dusty ivy. In the distance, pink and white, rise the turrets of the building that is now the home of the theatrical costumiers Nathan and Bermans. To the right, painted a severe cream and piled like the super-structure of an ocean liner, sails the superb bridgehead of the old Craven A factory in Mornington Crescent. I could see my bit of yard and the next, concrete-covered and featuring a bottle bank and a bicycle, and the one beyond that. The sky was grey all over and fitted like a pan lid. As you may have gathered, my part of town does not go in for landscape gardening, though we try, oh, how we try. Next door nurtures roses, man-sized cabbages, boy-sized Michaelmas daisies and family-size washing. On the other side we have a tasteful display of unpruned rubble, late-flowering piping, rampant old iron, and, until recently, set plumb in the middle of a squashed lawn, a rather rare specimen of a toilet bowl with seat. I myself have plastic poppies twined about the branches of a mountain ash, but I always bring them indoors at the first sign of frost.

You can therefore understand my astonishment yesterday when I saw a piano stool, a round one on three legs in the yard beyond the bottle bank, and a lady wearing a shady hat and white gloves sauntering among the fallen leaves towards it. Even as I watched she sat down and raised her gloved hands and began pumping her elbows up and down like bellows. She didn't have a piano, so I didn't bother to open the window, but she did have a halo round her head. As you may imagine I fairly raced downstairs to the kitchen where my daughter and the cleaner were shaking rugs out of the back window and arguing about men.

'There's no middle road,' my daughter was complaining, 'they either wear kid gloves or boxing gloves.'

'Ah, how sweet,' exclaimed the cleaner (she often gets the wrong end of the stick) when I'd described what I had just seen.

'So?' demanded my daughter. 'Are you trying to make out you've seen a ghost?'

She ran upstairs to see the apparition for herself, but, of course, the woman had disappeared. There followed a heated discussion both on the state of my mind and my lack of musical aptitude. My daughter also brought up the unfortunate time I arrived 'half-seas-over' to collect her from a piano lesson and insisted on playing the *Fairy Wedding Waltz*,

Miss Smith expires.

during which rendering I collapsed face downwards over the ivories.

'Oh, I never, little lamb,' I protested, which is what I always call her when I feel I'm being sacrificed. It did however remind me of the cautionary tale of my son's nursery school teacher, a lady named Miss Smith, referred to as Mith Mith by her lisping charges. It's a true story, albeit tragic. A group of infants on a Tuesday morning just before Christmas in a house in Ullet Road, Liverpool, were discovered at home-time marching up and down swigging bottles of milk in an abandoned manner while Mith Mith lay slumped across the piano. She had been dead for a quarter of an hour and had apparently passed on in the middle of *The Grand Old Duke of York*. This shocking incident has remained fresh as a daisy in the memory because I hadn't got round to paying the fees, whereas the rest of the mothers had stumped up the three guineas a term in advance.

Neither the cleaner nor my daughter would believe a word of it. As I could no more prove the existence of that ghost of Christmas past than I could produce the lady in the back yard, I went upstairs in a huff to consult the *Oxford Companion to the Mind,* an excellent work of scholarship edited by Richard Gregory, which no girl should be without. It didn't say much about ghosts except that they're manifestations of dead persons in human form, and that sometimes the person who sees one is in a state of fear or guilt. I'm now quite satisfied I saw Mith Mith, summoned up by that snatch of music heard at the traffic lights.

I'm thinking of slipping out tonight and throwing a cheque over the garden wall so that the poor soul can rest in peace.

22. Health of the nation

The Council did make cuts in the library services and have continued to do so. Five years on, local libraries have thrown out so many good books and stocked their shelves with such an abundance of rubbish that it scarcely matters whether they close altogether.

I don't think people over the age of forty-five should wear jeans, hold hands in the street or be seen jogging in the park. Anything in shorts – unless it's a child – and running into the bargain, makes me feel very uneasy. Nor can I bear the way some politicians often trip in and out of a camera shot linking fingers with their wives as though fearful they'll topple over without support.

Ron and Nancy [Reagan] do it all the time, but then, he almost certainly would fall over without her, and besides, any sort of behaviour is permissible after the age of eighty. I haven't the slightest objection to 80-year-olds in jeans holding hands and jogging.

Another thing I don't like to see exhibited in middle-age is political conviction. Surely that sort of nonsense is best left to the young and to members of Parliament? When I was twenty I was picked to hassle the American Embassy in Liverpool, my baby son as a prop on my hip, to protest against Kennedy doing something or other in the Bay of Pigs. I was so enamoured of the Ambassador – he was probably only a consul – that, far from arguing, I agreed with everything he said.

A few months later I went off to London, by coach, on a delegation consisting of the Workers of Liverpool, to join in a march to the House of Commons. On arrival at Victoria I rushed to the phone to inquire whether my infant son had pined away during my absence, and by the time I returned to the cafeteria everybody had disappeared. I never set eyes on my delegation again until we met up for the return journey. I spent my dinner money on a taxi, which was a dead loss seeing that the streets were choked with thousands of the common man chanting 'Two, four, six, eight, Handley Page have locked the gate.' When I finally caught up with the queue in the court-yard a man from Glasgow pointed at Big Ben and shouted 'I canna abide time. When I'm in power I'll pull down that wee tower with ma bare hands.' I thought he was absolutely right.

When you're young you want to pull down the lot, whether you're part of it or not. Perhaps it has something to do with hormones. When you're old, you scratch your head and notice the pattern of the bricks. Nobody who endures a so-called normal experience of life ends up believing that either Left or Right has the single solution. Years may rot our teeth, dim our eyes, quench the spring in our step, but they sure as heck teach us that there are two sides to every question, if not ten, and that what appeared expedient in youth may well in later years be revealed as folly. But then, we are what we are, a sum total of environment, temperament and upbringing.

I'm going on about this because last week I attended a meeting at the Hampstead Town Hall to protest against the proposed cuts in library services in Camden. It was extremely well attended and most of those present could be described as middle-aged. I myself arrived in a state of geriatric shock having extinguished a fire in the kitchen – I fell asleep while boiling potatoes – before leaving the house. There were some impassioned speeches along the lines of 'Give us back our books, heritage of the people', etc., but nobody came to blows. Indeed the audience was remarkable for its 'two sides to every question' attitude. No sooner had it been agreed that the libraries were essential to the Health of the Nation than it was disclosed that hardly anyone approved of the various branches being increasingly stocked with videos and pop records. No sooner had we voiced our disapproval that 150 library 'workers' were in danger of losing their jobs than we questioned the necessity for employing so many in the first place.

Having reiterated that life would be poorer without access to good literature, many of us admitted that it was difficult to find works in this category readily available on the shelves. The murdered playwright Joe Orton believed that, far from nourishing the populace, the libraries produced a diet of pap and mush. He was so incensed at his Islington branch failing to stock a copy of *The Decline and Fall of the Roman Empire* that he defaced the jackets of lesser books and substantially raised the expectations of readers of Dorothy L. Sayers by incorporating the word 'knickers' in the blurb of one of her novels. He went to prison for it, though these days he might well have got off with a fine and a recommendation that he should take up journalism.

The seasoned rate-payers of Camden left the Town Hall fully determined to fight the proposed closures, with the added proviso that the whole organisation of the libraries should be looked into. You see what maturity can do for one. By all means hold fast to what one believes in but never let conviction close the book.

Footnote. I have received a debilitating note from Dr M Rosen of Kensington, who tells me that he has great sympathy for my dead father and that my personality probably 'sent him to an early grave'. He also accuses me of living too much in the past. What I need, he says, 'is a healthier attitude to life', and he suggests I go for runs in the park. It's kind of him to be worried about my well-being, but I do assure him that my Dad died at a perfectly respectable age after getting into a temper over backing the car down the path.

23. The finest mothers

The morning after my unfortunate tangle with the table I rang the British Telecom archives and asked for information on the lady speaking-clock of my youth, her who was always known as 'the girl with the golden voice'. They were very helpful and I subsequently wrote a novel about a young girl, abandoned at birth, who knew that her mother was the speaking-clock and kept ringing her up to hear her tell the time.

The other evening I tripped over a pile of books in my living room and knocked myself out on the edge of the table. I know I came to in a pool of blood because I had to mop it up later. I went downstairs with the curious intention of ringing the Nat West for help, but I couldn't get my brain around any telephone numbers and was outraged when some fool kept telling me the time by Accurist. Who needs to know the time at a *time* like that! In the end my neighbour arrived – apparently I had got through to one of my daughters – and she was very kind and efficient. Two days later the people over the road told me some woman had phoned them in the middle of the night, twice in fact, uttered the words, 'Good evening, is the bank manager at home?' and replaced the receiver.

I recount this pathetic story simply to illustrate the fact that into the brightest life a little rain must fall, and that the subconscious moves in a mysterious way its wonders to perform. You see, I had been wandering about my room trying to decide what I should write for this column, and in falling over I had displaced the one book among many whose contents admirably fill the bill for this particular week. I do believe I have stumbled across the answer to a dilemma in which many mothers find themselves these

The time sponsored by Accurist ...

days, and I am anxious to share my knowledge. Only the other week my fellow columnist Irma Kurtz was in despair when her beloved son was home for the hols. (In case you've forgotten, he made a bit of a mess; he didn't wash up.) Oh dear! What expectations we nurture, what intentions we harbour! Let me say at once that it can all be sorted out with the help of *Cassell's Household Guide* for 1912. This admirable volume untangles all those little vexations of everyday life; stewing kippers in a paper bag; planting a fir tree in the hall among whose branches yellow canaries may build their nests and fly about at leisure.

No less a personage than Chief Scout Robert Baden-Powell did exactly this in his London home, and Mrs Powell comments that it was a marvellous ice-breaker at dinner parties. Further advice is given on the renovation of gas mantles whose burner holes have been ruthlessly enlarged; the waving of hair without damage; the supervision of the household donkey, tweeny and gardener. Last, but not least, under the heading of 'Womanhood at its Best', and subtitled 'The Hand of the Ruler', the management of sons. The author of this last welcome chapter is anonymous, unsung. It could well have been the Countess of Aberdeen, who edited the series. (I once knew a countess, an ex-theatre sister from Liverpool, who messed up my kitchen while trying to decapitate her husband, the Earl.) Whatever the identity of the author, she was undoubtedly possessed of that rare good sense and breeding essential to the upbringing of male off-spring glimpsed for a brief moment before the sounding of the dinner gong.

She observes: 'I have noticed on my travels through life that the finest mothers of my acquaintance, those who have easily moulded their sons to a perfection of physical, moral and intellectual manhood, have generally been failed women whom a superficial looker-on would have ruled out of court as a capable manager of stirring boys.' Tipping the scales at 8 st 4 lbs, I often murmur how true that is. 'A mother,' the author continues, 'who, when faced with a sullen boy, allows her temper to get away with her, snaps the chain of government, sells her birthright for a mess of porridge.' On reading this over I think the word should be pottage. 'The world is full of wholesome interests, and any boy possessed of the light of reason can surely be guided by a good mother away from gutter and sewer. Secure in his manhood he will regard his mother as a pal and they will sometimes be found together in the drawing-room. Here, with studied roughness the son will often fling an arm around mother's neck.'

This last paragraph is sympathetically illustrated by a photograph of a young man sporting a centre parting and balanced on the arm of a wicker chair in which Mother sits nervously crocheting table mats. He does look fairly studious. But Mamma, who bears a striking resemblance to Les Dawson, wears a rather fierce expression, grim of mouth and popping of eye; to be fair, this probably has something to do with the half-nelson applied to her Adam's apple. I must admit I was puzzled by the reference to 'studied roughness'. In my experience such skills come naturally. The author concludes her article with a mention of flags. There is much unfurling, exposure, brandishing and unsheathing of the things. Sometimes, sadly, far from standing up bravely, the flag flutters feebly in the parlour. I suspect this is mother's fault. 'There will possibly come a time when, in the face of sore temptation of the world, the flesh and the devil, the memory of the flag thus hoisted between them will stand between a son and temptation.'

Well, there you have it, and I'm only sorry that my own children are, alas, too old to gain the benefit of my new-found wisdom. However, I'm just going out to buy a canary.

24. A rum Sunday

I recommend going to the pictures twice in one day. It has the same effect as alcohol, and is possibly cheaper.

I spent Sunday with my daughter, her young man and the cleaner, and I must say it was an education. We had just finished lunch at about 3.30 when my daughter decided we should go to the pictures to see *Fatal Attraction*. It's years since I last went to the cinema and I was amazed at the size of the screen. The opening shot was of the skyline of New York and it was so realistic and so beautiful to look at that I wondered why people write books any more. I mean, how can one possibly match in words the camera's panoramic depiction of a city? I felt quite depressed.

The film was chugging on quite normally – man meets girl, takes her out to dinner, sees her home, etc. – when quite suddenly they both lost all sense of decorum and indulged in an orgy of passion in the kitchen, balanced on the edge of the cooker, to be exact. I gave an involuntary yelp of shocked protest and was told to shush by those on either side; and the cleaner hit me with her hat.

Later, the actors went through the same sort of carry-on in a lift in a warehouse. The odd thing was that there was a perfectly adequate bed in this girl's apartment. I now see why, on TV at least, everyone's sheets and pillow-cases are whiter than driven snow. Obviously, beds have gone out of fashion with the young.

We had no sooner come out into the windy night than my daughter said there was another film she wanted to see in Leicester Square. I did feebly remark that two cinemas in one day seemed rather decadent, but was swept along in the general enthusiasm. What followed was an eye-opener. We had two hours to pass before the film began so we wandered

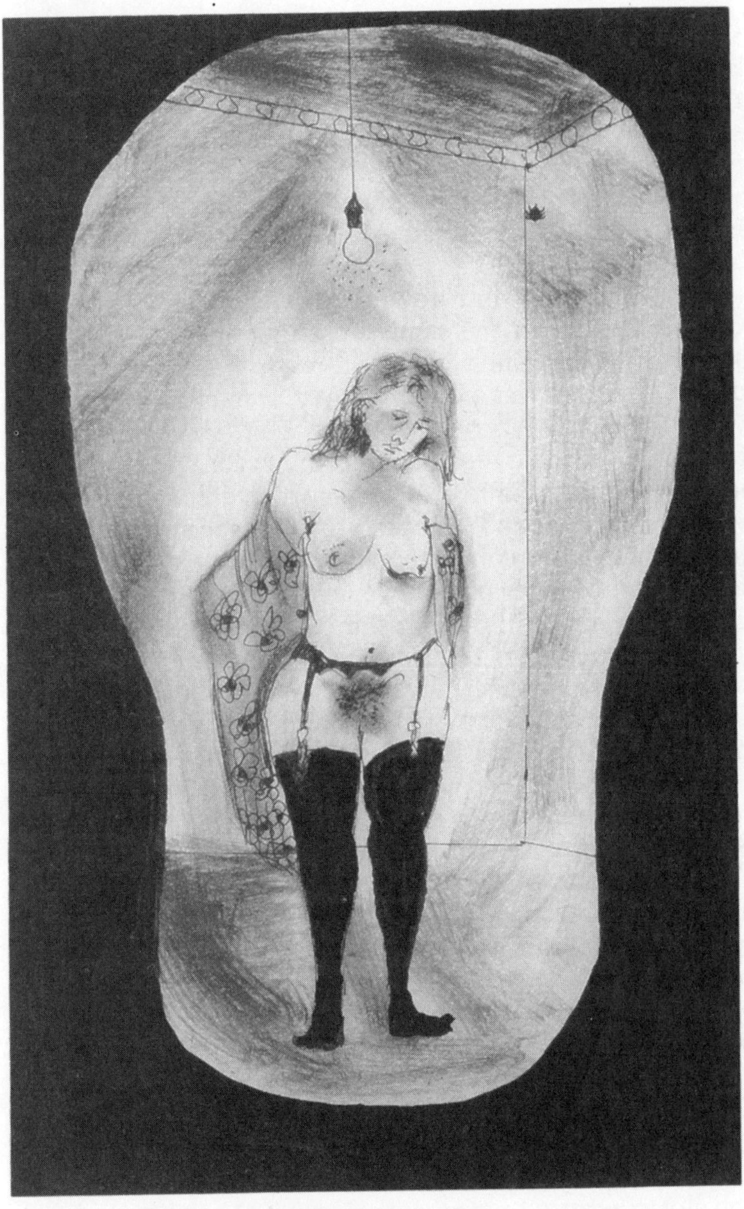

Through the keyhole.

through Chinatown. Here we visited a supermarket where I bought a fly whisk and a bag of pickling onions. It was then that the cleaner, spying some lurid electric signs advertising strip shows and the like, hared off down a side street. We followed, peering nervously into dimly-lit interiors whose walls were decorated with pictures of ladies photographed in that state always referred to by an earlier generation as the 'altogether'.

We walked up and down several times until, like Mr Gladstone, and in the same crusading spirit of social research, we determined to take a closer look at the seamy side of life. As there was possibly safety in numbers – I myself was particularly worried about the white slave traffic – the four of us handed over a pound coin each to a man in a black leather vest and climbed some very dirty steps to a room. It was terribly dark and I couldn't find my spectacles; I had to have help to fit the coin in the slot. I found myself in a cubicle with a sort of letter box at eye level which opened on to a bare room not unlike a hamster cage. Inside stood a stout pale girl in a black nightie scratching at the mark of a hypodermic on her arm. She ran forward, wagged a disapproving finger at me, mouthed that two in a box was against the rules, and then the letter box flap closed again. That was it.

We went two doors up and this time were foolish enough to part with £2 each to see 'a man and a woman in bed'. Armed with my fly whisk I had descended half way down the stairs when we were swept back up again by a group of disgruntled businessmen who shouted that it was 'all a racket'. Buying drinks at vastly inflated prices was obligatory, they said, and, worse, they were spiked with an unknown chemical that induced palpitations of the heart and weakness of the knees.

The film at the Odeon was very well done – all about the CIA, and starring Gene Hackman. Here again the action was threaded by love-making, always in the back of a moving taxi. The young lady laughed a lot. I couldn't concentrate on the story because I was wondering why in this age of permissiveness there was still a demand for the sort of squalid spectacle to be found in Soho. I can understand the motives of the girls involved: they are presumably in it for the money. But what breed of men, in surroundings musty with the stench of old air-raid shelters, can possibly find excitement in watching through peep holes the pathetic pretence of self-arousal?

It was a rum Sunday, but it still wasn't over. When we came out into Leicester Square, we bought fish and chips, and as I was crossing the road a young man called me by name. He said he had just borrowed one of my books from the library; I offered him a chip. He said he'd rather have a bit of fish, and then he asked me if I had an envelope to put it in. Appalled at his obvious need to store food I was about to give him some money when he explained that he would keep the fish for ever if I'd autograph the envelope.

How daft can you get? I refused of course; the fish had been going off even before it was cooked.

Footnote. I received a very nice letter from a Mr Emerson, medical professions manager of Nat West Bank, who points out that I was on the right lines when I tried to ring the bank after bashing my head open in the middle of the night. I now have a direct line number, though I hope I won't have need of it. I don't think there are any extra charges.

25. Minnie and Winnie

This is a much sadder article than it appears; to me, that is. I hadn't known, until Minnie told me, that my mother had been hoping to marry the Major. He wasn't a major, of course, but now I look back she did talk about him a lot.

Minnie and Winnie both lived in Formby, the village I grew up in. Minnie still does. Winnie was my mother and Minnie is my brother's mother-in-law. Actually, she isn't any more, because my brother too is dead. Last week I stayed with Minnie after giving a talk to the Formby Arts Society. I'm quite used to going round the country chatting about my past and the place I lived in, but I felt a bit inhibited talking to people who knew me when I was young. Quite a few times I was heckled for getting things wrong.

I said the contraption that used to trundle up the lane carrying the contents of the cesspits from the cottages beyond the railway line was known as the Lavender Cart. Everyone disagreed and said it was called the Marmalade Cart. The horse, I said, went by the name of Murgatroyd. Wrong, they shouted. It was Bruce. I think I was right because at the time Tommy Handley and Ronald Frankau had a double act known as Murgatroyd and Winterbottom, and that's how the horse got its name. In any case, who's ever heard of a horse called Bruce?

Lots of matronly ladies kept coming up to me and saying things like: 'You know who I am, don't you? You must do, you knocked me into the Alt canal when I was seven.'

'Go on, put a name to the face. You remember, you threw my school panama out of the train window.'

The only person I did remember was a tall, freckled girl whose father had worn a flat cap and kept greyhounds. She was still tall and freckled and her eyes had remained the same. It's odd how eyes don't change while the rest of us fades.

Afterwards I went home with Minnie and a friend called Eunice, who used to live next door to my mother. We had a long chat about Winnie. She and Minnie were what you might term bosom enemies. The rivalry between them was fierce. If audition night for the Amateur Dramatic Society was on a Thursday, then Winnie was sure to ring Minnie to tell her not to forget they were casting for *Bill of Divorcement* on Friday. When the Wine Society telephoned Minnie to say they needed a new committee member and would she please contact Winnie – my mother was never in – Minnie would confide she knew for a fact that Winnie was too busy to accept such a position and why not ask Betty Rimmer. When Winnie heard about it she'd get on the phone to all her cronies and announce, 'She's done it again.'

And then there was the time they both went on the trip with the Wine Society to the Rhone Valley. Betty Rimmer went too. Winnie picked up a man called Gunter and Betty Rimmer chummed up with a man called Ernie from Hartlepool. Then Ernie changed his mind and took a fancy to Minnie, and Betty Rimmer pinched Gunter off Winnie. It was Betty Rimmer's baby-doll pyjamas that did it. Winnie was in tears the next morning. She told everyone that Betty had 'done it again'.

I asked Eunice and Minnie if they thought my mother really did carry on with men, or was it just innocent flirtation, a longing for attention?

Minnie gave me an old-fashioned look.

'Well,' said Eunice, 'Bert from over the line used to arrive every Friday afternoon without fail and stay for two hours. Your mother said he was bringing her prawns. And she certainly set her cap at that fellow who played a Beefeater in the panto, even if she did say his lance was too small.'

'And it broke her heart,' said Minnie, 'when that Major married Bunty Hargreaves from the Bridge club. She rang everybody up and complained that Bunty had done it again.'

Then there was the time when Eunice's daughter was

getting married and Winnie offered to put up one of the overspill. He was only a young chap yet he sent Winnie a bunch of red roses for weeks afterwards. You don't do that for a pot of tea and an electric blanket. 'But we never caught Winnie actually in bed with anyone, did we?' asked Eunice, and Minnie said no, not actually in bed.

I couldn't help feeling things had changed. Minnie is well over eighty and for a good seventy years she would never have dreamed of expressing herself so freely on such a delicate subject. It felt strange listening to the two of them, as if I'd never known my own Mum. The sad thing is I think I knew her well enough to believe that she had probably sent the roses to herself. I hope I'm wrong.

Footnote. Melanie Gage of Shoebury Road, East Ham, writes '... I have been an avid reader of yours since finding a discarded copy of *The Dressmaker* on a southbound Northern Line tube some years ago ... The other day on my homeward journey on the Central Line I was quietly strap-hanging, deep in *Mum and Mr Armitage,* when a loud voice accosted me and accused me of being in possession of a book by that dreadful woman who writes in the *Standard.* "Filthy rubbish," he cried. "Pure trash." '

I don't at all mind the gentleman's comments, Melanie, but I am a bit miffed about your finding my book 'discarded'. The same thing happened a few months ago when someone told me he had found no fewer than four of my books abandoned on the Piccadilly Line. Damn it, they can't all be that uninteresting.

26. Tricks of memory

I have always been interested in memory. Why, for instance, can very old people, who haven't a clue about what happened yesterday, remember in detail an event experienced sixty years before? I suppose it could be that in one's seventh or eighth decade nothing in the preceding twenty years is worth remembering, let alone the previous day.

Two days ago I switched on the wireless just in time to catch an interesting discussion on the subject of memory. 'What is it?' someone asked Professor Richard Gregory. 'How does it work?' The professor proceeded to tell him, and it was riveting stuff. Apparently the brain lays down chemical tracks – tyre marks in the mud, so to speak – and information is then stored in the circuit system. People who get hit over the head can't remember what happened in the minutes before the blow because they don't have time to make tracks.

There are certain people, a very few, who suffer torments from having too good a memory. A poor chap in Russia was mentioned who had a terrible time when crossing the road. His storage circuit was so good that he projected images of heavy traffic even before he set foot in the gutter. You see his problem – he could never be sure whether he was avoiding real cars or the ones he had dodged the day before. He actually had to train himself to be forgetful, which feat he accomplished by writing down memories on a piece of paper and then setting fire to the paper. In his mind, you understand. I have doubts whether this would be a satisfactory solution, because surely he would only be replacing one memory with another. Let's suppose he was trying to forget a 24 bus to Hampstead Heath. Instead of an ordinary bus he'd now have a burning bus.

Professor Gregory went on to explain that in any case all

memory is fictional, which is why autobiographical accounts, and historical ones, for that matter, are notoriously inaccurate. We censor memories by recalling only those fragments we wish to remember.

Now it happens that I spent the weekend with friends in a cottage in Sussex, taking healthy walks through a landscape littered with trees torn from the ground on the night of the Great Storm. I have always thought of trees as wooden things that stick up out of the grass, and was staggered to see how different they look when lying down. For one thing they leave huge craters filled with muddy water which bear a curious resemblance to the holes left in the skin when a boil bursts. This is, of course, a personal observation, and perhaps owes something to my bedside reading, while in the country, of Defoe's *Journal of the Plague Year*. Did you know that at the height of the Plague, in September, people died at the rate of a thousand a day? Defoe fills an entire chapter with descriptions of the various boils and swellings, some hard, some soft, that heralded death. I dwell on these unpleasant details to illustrate the fragmented aspect of memory, for I now realise that it was not Defoe that turned the trees into eruptions but a much earlier recollection that shot through my circuits while listening to the radio discussion. The presenter of the programme was chuntering on about electrical impulses, etc., when suddenly the name Leslie Welch came up. Instantly I was at home, forty years before, sitting in the kitchen listening to the voice of Welch on the wireless while my father applied a red-hot kaolin poultice to the boil on my brother's neck. For those of you who won't or can't remember the name, Leslie Welch was known as the Memory Man. His speciality was sport. He could reel off winners of the Derby and cricket scores, and who beat Everton in 1927, and all without taking a breath. Anyway, he's not terribly relevant; it's what he did to my circuits that is interesting, at least to me.

The way I see it, I was already half remembering boils before reading Defoe and noticing the trees. The Memory Man merely plugged in the connection. Nor do I think I've

'Bend over, lad, and let me get at that boil.'

fictionalised my brother's boils, or his carbuncles for that matter, though these days they seem to have gone out of fashion, which is odd because we're always being told of the dangers of junk food and how much healthier our diet was during rationing. You look at the neck of any man over the age of 50 and you'll see the scars left behind. I had a boil up my nose on my wedding day, which accounts for the painful smile in the photographs. What bothers me is what I've chosen to forget of the scene in the kitchen. It would seem, on the surface, to be extraordinarily detailed; the calendar on the wall with the photograph of the Avondale Tin Plate factory in Wales and the black circle round 9 September; the adhesive tape holding Dad's spectacles together as he bends over my brother at the kitchen table; the little flame of reflected firelight dancing across the dial of the wireless.

Is there anything to be made of the encircled date, seeing that the Plague was at its height in that month, albeit 300 years before? I leave you with this scientific problem. What lurks behind the boil?

Footnote. Last week, L.J. Liddy of Dagenham complained in the correspondence columns of the *Standard* of my excessive use of the personal pronoun. He wrote: 'B.B.'s use of "I" is infuriating. I counted eight "I"s in one 25-word paragraph.' You're absolutely right, Mr Liddy, and one appreciates your point of view, but, oh dear, one is now in an awful pickle as to how one can remedy the matter. One will try harder in future. Can one say more?

27. Second edition

Brian Masters and I were both working on books about murderers. He was still in contact with his, Dennis Nilsen; mine, poor old John Selby Watson, headmaster of Stockwell Proprietary Grammar School, who beat his wife to death with a horse-pistol, was long since dead (1884). I expect Nilsen has a number. Watson's was Y 1395.

Have you ever seriously thought about turning-points in life? Real turning-points, not just the time the dog got run over or the day you discovered how to tie shoelaces.

Last week I took part in a series called *Second Edition*, which goes out live on Radio Four on a Saturday afternoon. Each week the subject is different, but the format is the same, consisting of a discussion between Kevin Mulhern and two invited guests, interspersed with recordings from the BBC archives. It's a very clever idea. There is nothing more compelling than unedited chat spiked with voices from the past. Think about it. Everything today is rehearsed, added to, coloured, rehashed, from political comment to personal tragedy to the food we eat. A televised version of the Royals arriving home after that skiing tragedy, men in front, women behind, walking two by two, is an edited version of reality. They did walk like that at one moment, but there was another moment when it was different. The editor, like a good nanny, chose which moment, in accord with sentimental, conventional behaviour, was best thought to illustrate respect. I'm not knocking it, but how can one take as immediate the vision of the Royal ladies all in black? I know the colour is in fashion, but nobody dresses up for death any more – except politicians.

I digress. A live radio programme is a different matter altogether. If the broadcaster is as drunk as a skunk, or the comedian's patter as blue as the summer sky, little can be done about it. It's something to do with air space. There was a famous occasion when a chap called Lasky, a sort of poor man's Richard Dimbleby, in a Brahms and Liszt condition described a review of the Navy. It was a rum commentary in every sense of the word and became known as the 'Fleet's Lit Up' broadcast. Lasky was never heard of again. Frankie Howerd, overstepping the suggestive mark, was sent into the wilderness for years. By an odd coincidence, in the middle of writing this, Sam Brittan, speaking live on television, has just made a blistering attack on Mrs Thatcher. There's no mistaking the real thing; it leaves one breathless.

Anyway, *Second Edition* last week was all about turning-points. Kevin Mulhern asked Brian Masters and me to discuss those events, both historical and personal, which we considered had affected us. First, we listened to earlier recordings – Eden on Suez, the announcement of the dropping of the atom bomb, Nehru on the British giving up India, Macmillan's 'Wind of Change' speech. Brian and I were a little anxious at the start, neither of us being too hot on political issues. I remembered the dropping of the bomb but had missed India – we weren't too bothered about the Empire up North. Then Brian told a story of how as a schoolboy he had written to the then mega-star Gilbert Harding, and how Harding had invited him round and thus influenced the rest of his life.

Much later the murderer Dennis Nilsen provided another turning-point, in that Brian subsequently visited him in prison in order to write his book on the case, *Killing for Company*. We listened to a home-videotape of Nilsen complaining about the seedy condition of his rented accommodation. 'The ceiling's unsafe,' he protested. 'It could fall and kill somebody.'

As for me, I thought my life had been grossly affected by viewing as a child the unexpurgated version of the footage taken by the Allied troops when they first entered Belsen. That, and the death of my mother.

It was surprising how many turning-points we managed

to fit in – the Pill, the homosexuality bill, the invention of the railways, Vietnam, Darwinism and any amount of revolutions including the French, Russian and Industrial. Oh yes, and man's first step on the moon. After our particular broadcast we were so relieved it was over without our actually having disgraced ourselves that Brian and I went a bit over the top while waiting for a taxi and planned a double-act series for television. Just him and me and a guest – well, more of a friend really – discussing very personal moments. I think this was brought on by memories of the Gilbert Harding interview with John Freeman when Gilbert started crying.

The idea of two interviewers is a good one and it hasn't been done before. And it wouldn't be like Wogan or Aspel – definitely no film stars or celebrities, not unless we could persuade them to appear in a 'Fleet's Lit Up' condition – just ordinary people talking about the time the dog got run over or the day they learned to tie their shoelaces.

Footnote. I received an excellent letter – slightly marred by the slogan 'Jesus is Unemployed' on the envelope – from Trevor Artingstoll of Romford regarding my article two weeks ago about the Palestinians. He says: 'It is a common mistake to attempt to quantify evil. To do so is like describing someone as being slightly pregnant. Evil is evil is evil. Do not despair at the fallibility of your political analysis. Dostoevsky was a political cretin after all.'

28. Saints and sinners

I'm not surprised that the cleaner and my children were upset by Death of a Salesman. I suspect that if the play gets revived and I take my grandchildren to see it, they too, being without a father, will fight back tears. We all want our Dads to be heroes, protectors of the weak, and it's just no good if they fail to oblige. Mrs Loman loved him, though; which is unusual. 'Attention must be paid,' she said.

I spent a pleasant Easter lunching with friends, reading the Sunday papers, buying second-hand books, looking at photographs, re-reading Arthur Miller's *Death of a Salesman*, and pottering through garden centres.

I bought a statue for the back yard – she's rather a shy lady wearing a revealing shift and I've christened her Willy Loman after the hero in *Death of a Salesman* – three pots of blue asters, one creeping thyme intended to kill off the weeds, and a cutting of ivy which in time, I hope, will twine round Willy Loman and merge her into the background. At the moment she's gleaming against the grimy wall like an advertisement for washing powder. On second thoughts, the photographs I looked at – taken by David Newman and on show at Birch and Conran, Dean Street – excellent though they are, hardly come under the heading of 'pleasant'. 'Disturbing' would be a better word.

The exhibition, personally speaking, is dominated by a print of four embryos joined to the same floating placenta, navels bulging like dahlia tubers, knees bent as though jumping from a trampoline, bony hands outstretched and all suspended in a glass bottle laconically labelled 'Homo'. What an accident life is, what a casual affair! Auden, or someone like that, wrote a poem about it, something to do with the absurdity of planning anything. The gist of it is that the most suitable parents coming from the most favourable backgrounds often produce ill-favoured offspring, and vice versa. There's a particular line about a coupling in a ditch on a windy night ... *Two strangers flung together* ... tee-tum, tee-tum ... *And willy-nilly born he was, divinely formed and fair.*

In Liverpool, after the war, it was an ordinary sight to see children, in winter, walking barefoot, dressed in rags, legs pin-pricked with the marks of bug bites, hair shaved against the lice. When such urchins boarded a tram, the other occupants huddled together and stopped breathing to avoid the stench. Nobody really thought much could be done about the verminous poor. Why, if you gave them a decent bathroom they'd only keep the coal in it. Class, then, was obvious and readily accepted. Bless the Squire and his relations, keep us in our proper stations. There was royalty, who dressed their children in drab tweed coats and ankle socks and gave up beheading their wives in favour of stamp-collecting; the upper classes, whose sons were wrenched from Nanny and sent off to boarding schools and who later took their revenge shooting birds and running the country; the middle-class who felt guilty at doing so well and who stirred up revolutions; the poor who went on scratching, for a living as much as to relieve the itching. And all these classes threw up people of note: scientists and astronomers, artists, reformers and essayists, explorers and inventors. There were as many good men as bad, and who's to say which class produced more sinners than saints?

You could hardly call Willy Loman – the character in Arthur Miller's play, not the statue in my garden – a saint, but then you couldn't call him a sinner either. He was just an ordinary Joe trying to sell silk stockings and cotton reels, and when he died hardly anyone came to his funeral. When he was alive his wife told his sons that he mustn't be allowed to fall into his grave like an old dog. Attention must be paid, she said. He loved his son, Biff, and tried to make him all the things he hadn't been – brave, clever, good at baseball, a man's man and a woman's dream. Biff loved him back, until, turning up unannounced at a seedy hotel where he knew

Willy was staying, he discovered him in bed with a one-night stand. It wasn't so much the half-dressed woman that shocked him, but the fact that Willy had given her three packets of silk stockings, while, out of necessity, his wife went bare-legged. Willy committed suicide, after he had paid the last instalment on his apartment, so that his family could get the insurance.

I saw *Death of a Salesman* with Paul Muni in the lead. I was embarrassed because my father was a commercial traveller and had a suitcase full of little cotton bags bulging with corks, and I thought it was all about him. I remember I had a lump in my throat and when my mother asked if I was enjoying the play I told her to shut up. It was either that or burst into tears.

Some years back the play was revived with Warren Mitchell as Willy. I took my children and some of their friends, including the cleaner (then aged 15), to see it. The set was different but Mr Mitchell was better than Mr Muni. The children all wept, and the cleaner grew hysterical. She kept moaning. She was always hypersensitive: it shows in her dusting.

Afterwards, when we talked about it, they all said it reminded them of their fathers, and none of them had Dads who were salesmen. Come to that, none of them had Dads who actually lived with them, and most of them had Dads who lived with other women. It wasn't silk hosiery they had to contend with, but the more durable gift of sons and daughters. I think, probably, the play has more to do with love than insurance. The children all agreed that mothers and fathers had to be pruned, torn up, if the next generation was to flourish: and yet, being flesh of their flesh, the children felt torn apart at the discarding. In a roundabout way, that's why I bought the ivy for the lady statue in the garden. Apart from her whiteness, I felt she needed something to cling to. Which brings me back to that photograph of those half-developed babies drifting from the same placenta. Impossible to say what they might have become, to which class they might have belonged, if born. I've no idea how old they are, in the sense of how long they've been trapped in that glass jar. Seventy years, possibly. All the same, I have the uncomfortable thought that if they had gone to term – in spite of disease, of class, the lack of heart transplants and hip replacements, the vagaries of chance – they might well have lived fuller lives than those born tomorrow.

I think that every generation, no longer young, believes that the one before had an edge on things. Be that as it may, don't you often get the feeling that you're something of a specimen, anchored to God knows what, waiting for life before death?

29. Hosepipe

This is only about me turning the hose on my father in the garden when I was five years old. I don't know why I've remembered it so vividly. He hopped up and down a lot and cursed me, but he wasn't really cross.

In the middle of Sunday lunch at tea-time on Monday, during a furious discussion on AIDS and the National Front, Charlie came running in from the back yard, dripping wet. We asked if it was raining and he said, no, it was just that Darling Bertie had turned the hosepipe on him. One is forced to admire Bertie. He's not reached his fifth birthday and yet only last week he mended the lavatory seat. That job, however, was child's play, in a manner of speaking, compared with fitting the hose to the water supply. I don't have one of those male-female attachments, and how he managed to ram the end of the hose up the bath tap is a mystery. I was about to go down into the yard to congratulate him when the phone rang. It was a friend of mine, returned from a weekend in Avignon and anxious to hand on a hot newsflash should I be short of an item for this column.

Apparently, Le Pen, that pain who is leader of the French National Front, has ordered his nasty supporters to abstain from voting in the forthcoming election. It's a sort of protest against the unsuitability of Chirac, who's the chap who's standing against Mitterrand. My friend saw these two haranguing each other on French television, and she said both of them had intriguing mannerisms. Every time Chirac was asked a question he smiled broadly, as though he was listening to a joke. My friend found it very irritating. On the other hand, Mitterrand kept raising one eyebrow in a contemptuous manner. Far from finding this annoying, my friend waxed lyrical on how attractive it was. She said he had lovely high cheekbones and looked amazingly handsome for a man of seventy. She was just about to unravel, for my benefit and yours, the intricacies of the French political system and explain who stood for what, when something happened which caused my own eyebrow to rise. Bertie had staggered up the back steps and was pointing the hose towards me. I tried to tell his mother that he was watering the hall, but she was too busy arguing about Right-wing tendencies. I did attempt to tell Bertie where he had gone wrong and he was quite understanding about it. We took the hose down into the yard again, where he couldn't resist filling up my right shoe. I was about to get cross when I remembered a hot day in summer when I'd done the same thing to the turn-up of his great-grandfather's trousers. He hadn't found it funny either, but he didn't say anything because the garden was full of uniformed men dozing on deckchairs and the grass.

The soldiers were members of the British Expeditionary Force who had been snatched from the Dunkirk beaches and landed up and down the coast. They'd come by lorry to Formby, not boat, from God knows where, and my father, alerted by loudspeaker, had collected two carloads of them from the church hall in the village. He wasn't supposed to have any petrol, and my mother was worried in case he was reported for black-market dealings, but he said that that would be the last thing, in the circumstances, on anybody's mind. It was all a little like that film in which Walter Pidgeon goes off in his pleasure boat to France and Mrs Miniver stays behind and captures a German pilot, only my mother boiled the kettle all day long instead. I wasn't allowed to pester anyone with questions. All I knew was that there'd been a battle; the soldiers in the garden were dead-tired and the rest of them were dead. One did give me some French coins before he was driven away to the station. He balanced them on his palm and told me to take care of them in memory of the day. Do you remember how huge and knotted men's hands were in the old days, even when they were young? You don't see hands like that any more, not unless they're Irish. We kept the coins in the left-hand drawer of my mother's sewing machine. Those were the days, and they continued for years after the war, when nobody knew anybody who travelled abroad, or was ever likely to. Not for fun. London was foreign, never mind France.

Back at the dinner-table the discussion about the National Front was still raging. The cleaner had been to Brick Lane the week before and seen an English contingent. She said they were very nicely spoken and had Union Jacks tattooed on their foreheads. I couldn't really concentrate because I was still trying to work out how NOT voting will get France where le Pen wants it to be. I thought his lot were all in favour of the smiling Chirac. Besides, I was too busy bailing out the paddling buffalo. Later, I tried to find the French coins to give to my grandchildren. Alas, unlike the memory of the day, they were lost and gone forever.

Footnote. Dear Mr Robertshaw: I spent a happy hour playing your composition, with one finger, on the piano. What a cheerful song it is, and how kind of you to compare me with Emily Brontë. I note that you sent the same song to Mr Michael Parkinson, but you never heard a dicky bird. Shame!

30. Intellectuals

I used to like the Brian Walden interviews. He treated his guests rather like a terrier hanging onto a bone. He was quite nice to Mrs Thatcher really, but he still wouldn't let go.

I have spent a lot of time since Sunday trying to find out what the word 'intellectual' means. Yes, I have looked it up in the dictionary and I must say it's easier to understand what intellectual isn't than what it is.

For instance, it's pretty difficult to be intellectual if you're vacuous, brainless or moronic, and next to impossible if you're animal, vegetable or mineral. Come to think of it, a good definition should mention bicycle clips. I know a bicycle clip in itself can't be classed as intellectual, but its wearer could be. Certainly the vicar of the parish in which I was born always wore them and he was considered one, an intellectual, I mean, because he had books in the house. So did my grandfather, two of them, both from the Everyman library, one on agnostics and the other to do with butterflies. People often said he should have taken Holy Orders, which is odd really because another definition of intellectual is non-spiritual. Of course, where I lived, such behaviour as the reading of books came under the general heading of airy-fairy, and if I'd thought of that earlier I'd have saved myself a lot of trouble. Airy-fairy, it seems to me, is a pretty apt description of the word in question.

All this waffle is leading me to the root cause behind my researches, mainly an article in the *Sunday Times* leisure section in which Brian Walden interviewed Mrs T on 'Why I Can Never Let Up'. On the whole, it was a good piece, spicy and informative and neither too impertinent nor too sycophantic. It was let down, however, by an absurd attack on John Mortimer, whom Mrs Thatcher castigated for being one of the airy-fairy brigade. Now I know that a paragraph can be taken out of context and its meaning destroyed, but it's not easy to distort the unconscious emphasis underlying the immediate response. At such moments, we are what we are, which is no more than the sum total of our domestic and historical background.

According to Brian Walden, Mrs Thatcher replied, in answer to a question why Mr Mortimer and other 'pinko writers' spoke so coldly of her, 'They have a terrible intellectual snobbery ... they think they have a talent and ability that none of the rest of the human race has.'

Admittedly Brian Walden's question was couched in curiously tactless terms: 'Why can't they say I don't believe in Thatcherism but I admit she's a vivacious old thing?' – if it had been me I really would have wielded the handbag – but her answer, or rather the feeling behind the words, is jolly interesting.

This country has not, in the last hundred years, produced a political leader who could be said to be the intellectual equal of Pitt, Gladstone or Disraeli. Such men had the benefit, for what it's worth, of a classical education. They were dotty about words. Why, in 1871, according to the *Dictionary of National Biography,* the entire Cabinet debated for days the exact meaning of a few lines of Latin scribbled by an obscure old schoolmaster who was on trial for the murder of his wife. Shortly afterwards, the study of the sciences usurped that of classics, and 'intellectual' as a term became debased. My grandfather, and I suspect Mrs T's father thought it referred to anyone who liked poetry, played the piano, grew a beard, subscribed to the *Statesman and Nation* and went out in odd socks.

'Revolutionary doctrines,' Mrs T observed, 'usually come from the ranks of intellectuals and academics.' I presume she means in the past. I've never thought of Arthur Scargill as being particularly intellectual, any more than I've lately noticed Professor Freddie Ayer running amok in Baker Street with his hammer and sickle. It might be a nice thing if Mrs Thatcher read *English History in Verse,* an anthology edited by her colleague Kenneth Baker, published by Faber and Faber. It is worth quoting a few lines from Mr Baker's introduction:

'It is important for people living today to understand how people came to be what they are, to understand the forces and events that have shaped the institutions which guide and govern us, and generally to recognise how our rich and complex past has shaped what we think of as our national identity.'

For those of you who think poetry is best left to long-haired pinkos, do persevere and have a go at this collection. It has some lovely things in it, from Shakespeare to Tennyson to Noel Coward. I particularly like Betjeman's lines on the arrest of Oscar Wilde:

He rose, and he put down the Yellow Book.
He staggered – and, terrible-eyed,
He brushed past the palms on the staircase
And was helped to a hansom outside.

Favourite, though, has got to be Mr Kipling, the poet not the baker:

When the Himalayan peasant meets the he-bear in his pride,
He shouts to scare the monster, who will often turn aside.
But the she-bear thus accosted rends the peasant tooth and nail,
For the female of the species is deadlier than the male.

31. Downright turpitude

The Almshouses referred to here are the same ones Dickens walked past as a boy. They're in Bayham Street. The boots, still in the window, were commissioned ten years ago. I paid a deposit to the cobbler and then never went back.

The weekend being fine I spent several minutes in the back yard attending to the estate. What with shoving the geranium tubs from one corner to another, and throwing slugs over the garden wall into next door's plot, I should have been worn out. But I wasn't. Trouble is, I have so small a patch and have so enthusiastically packed it with clumps of this and that, that there simply isn't any room left for improvement. I've pruned everything that moves a dozen times, and as I've scattered seeds over every inch, even on the concrete, I didn't dare weed in case I threw the baby out with the bath water. This being the case, I decided some time after lunch to pull up some orange things – wall-flowers perhaps – which I can't remember planting in the first place. The resulting heady expanse of virgin soil sent me hotfoot in the general direction of my local garden centre.

Those of you who are familiar with Camden Town will know what I mean when I say 'general', it being quite impossible on either a Saturday or a Sunday to go anywhere in a direct line owing to the thousands of visitors who zoom towards Camden Lock like bees to the hive. Accordingly I went up the side streets, past the cobbler's with my boots in the window – they've been there for five years now and I don't like to disturb them – past the magical meat boutique, the Greek bookshop and the kebab stall, and left by the Almshouses. It was here that I was greeted by a group of elderly gentlemen who were sitting on the ground having a little rest. After exchanging a few cordial quips I continued on my way and spent a pleasant hour buying a winter clematis, four pots of pansies, one of swan river daisies, and two pots of pinks, which, when I found my spectacles the next morning and read the label, turned out to be chives, and a bug gun. I had thoughtfully brought my shopping basket on wheels with me, and carefully stowing the plants inside I set off for home. I came back another route and ended up going through the pleasant churchyard at the back of the High Street. The tombstones, of course, have been ripped up, but the place does have a nice peaceful air about it. There are tulip beds and a lot of grassy mounds covered in daisies, and rustic hollows where small children beat each other over the head with plastic swords. On one such mound, enjoying a little liquid refreshment, sprawled the senior citizens I had encountered on my outward journey. Spying my winter clematis hoisted like an aerial above the buggy, they announced they were grand gardeners themselves. Sure, hadn't they grown their own veggies in the auld country? Didn't they have the green fingers and the thumbs to go with it? Would I not sit down and have a swig of the hard stuff?

It seemed churlish to refuse, seeing they were drinking, so they said, to the health of St Pancras and the downfall of Stafford. For a time, in my ignorance, I thought they were railway enthusiasts and that we were toasting stations, only for some reason, a missed connection perhaps, an unhappy experience under the clock in the booking hall, Stafford had been given the green thumbs down. As it turned out, Pancras really was a saint, a young one of fourteen who had been martyred on 12 May, AD 304, and Strafford, not Stafford, was the swine who had ruled Ireland with a rod of iron under Charles I, and met his comeuppance on Tower Hill on the same day of the month in 1641. The conversation was so stimulating that one scarcely noticed, after the first burning swig, the taste of the hard stuff, though I don't think I've ever swallowed anything quite like it before. I do remember there was no label on the bottle, and that its neck was wiped with an old sock every time it was handed to me, proving that my companions matched delicacy of feeling with a knowledge of history. What I don't remember is how I got home, or quite why I attacked the garden with such gusto.

Rebecca in the basement said that one moment I was on my knees in the front, digging up the flower bed like a mad dog and hurling pansies in all directions, and the next I was in the back yard, stamping up and down on the rockery and aiming the bug gun at the cat. The following day I found at least two foot of the winter clematis wound round the bath tap. The rest I'd planted rather firmly. None of the pansies had heads on them and there's no trace at all of the swan river daisies. I found the pinks in the fridge.

Later, I looked up Strafford in my *Book of Days*, and very interesting it was too. 'He was undoubtedly a great political culprit; yet the iniquitous nature of his trial and condemnation is equally undoubted. Political crime is always so mixed up with sincere, though blind, opinion that it seems hard to visit it with the punishment which we award to downright turpitude.'

Now, there's a word to conjure with. I wouldn't be at all surprised if it wasn't the stuff I was drinking in the churchyard.

32. Too much brass

I still feel shame at the afternoon I spent with Beryl Reid. For some reason I was sent for hours in advance and then given mugs of whisky. What with delays, heat and nerves, by the time the camera turned in my direction I was far from my best.

I had tea last week with Beryl Reid, in a baronial hall in the middle of a park. I was decked out in a hat belonging to my daughter and a fur tippet from Oxfam. Miss Reid wore an elegant dress of blue and black, and a peach of a hat with a gossamer veil. There was also a young man called Peter, straight out of *Entertaining Mr Sloane*, who was dressed from top to toe in very tight black leather.

We were gathered together for the television programme *Review* to discuss our feelings about the excellent paintings of Beryl Cook. The resulting conversation, or dialogue, as it is sometimes called, was free-ranging.

'I think Beryl likes putting upright poles in her work, don't you, Beryl?' 'Those are Beryl's phallic symbols, Beryl.'

Peter's job was to limp on with the canvases and put up with a lot of badinage much centred on the tightness of his trousers.

Miss Reid and I were both unstinting in our admiration of the other Beryl's art, and we particularly admired the painting of the ladies' stag night with the hussy in the green dress plucking at the gentleman stripper's G-string, but we had a difference of opinion over the keyhole picture. Actually, there were two of these, and the first presented no problem, being merely a study of a stout lady fresh out of the bath peering through the said keyhole. The second picture depicted what she saw. Miss Reid said it was obviously an orgy; I said it was a group of people in the rush hour on a bus that had drawn up too quickly and thrown everyone to the floor. Miss Reid said that was rubbish because you couldn't look at a bus through a keyhole, not when you'd just stepped out of a bath.

There was a lovely painting of a lady flasher exposing herself in a fur coat to a mild-looking gentleman in a bowler hat. We were undecided about the meaning of this one, and concluded it was either exactly what it seemed – a wealthy street-walker trying to attract attention – or an imaginative housewife meeting hubby on his way home from work and putting a little excitement back into the marriage. We had an outright difference of opinion over a painting of two cats on a table. Miss Reid loved it, and I thought it was boring, but then I'm not a tremendous cat lover, possibly because of the two I own, a mother called Pudding and her son, Gerald Duckworth. Both of them are approaching the end of their second decade and look set to outlast me, though Gerald is handicapped through falling on his head once too often. His mother keeps knocking him off the window ledge, sending him hurtling into the basement area. We did try fitting him with a kind of crash-helmet bonnet, but he won't wear it. I like both of them, in a lukewarm sort of way, and I wouldn't mind having Pudding stuffed once she's passed on, but I haven't left either of them so much as a dead budgie in my will.

Which is why my mind is still boggling over that man who earlier this week left almost 7 million to cat charities. The newspaper I read said that his friends and relatives were shocked at the news, which must be something of an understatement. I'm surprised he had any friends, though of course, one should never jump to conclusions. For all we know he had endowed several orphanages when younger and already made generous provision for his family. Perhaps he just thought enough was enough and wanted to be rid of the stuff. I'm not really interested in why he left his fortune to the Grimalkin brigade, but I am fascinated as to how it feels to have 7 million under the mattress. Did he enjoy the millions when he was middle-aged and only get tired of them when he was geriatric? Did he keep rushing out and buying more and more things, only to find the interest kept piling up and the investments kept doubling? After all, one can only eat one meal at a sitting, love one woman at a time, particularly if you're over eighty. Don't forget he was a self-made man, and he may have had memories of happier days when to have money was a pleasure rather than a responsibility. Did the final blow come when the Government reduced his income tax and effectively shoved another couple of million into his weary pocket? Was it then, when the system had beaten him, that he thought, to hell with it, the moggies can have it?

Whatever the reasons and however wasteful the gift, I rather approve of the sentiment behind the gesture. As my Auntie Nellie used to say, botching a biblical quotation: 'It's not quite as hard for a man with brass to enter the kingdom of heaven as it is for a camel to get through the eye of a darning needle, but it's just as uncomfortable.'

33. Tears and laughter

I'm a great fan of Barry Humphries. An Evening with the Dame was a great occasion, a cross between a flower show and a Nuremburg rally. As Edna, he is like my mother, only crueller. As Humphries he could be brother to George Melly.

You all know that phrase much used by mothers when dealing with boisterous children: 'There'll be tears before bedtime.' Well, the other day – Tuesday to be exact – the opposite happened. I was weeping before lunch and laughing at night, so much so that I woke up the following day feeling really frail, as if I had lived a lifetime in a few short hours.

After brekkie, I was wandering, as is my habit, round the estate, plucking the odd withered bud off the pansies, when I spied a little bird crouching beside a geranium pot. He, or she, was very fat and feathery, far too stout to have just fallen out of a nest, and was cheeping loud enough to wake the dead. I said the usual things, like 'Oooh' and 'Aaah' and 'Where's your Mum?', and then I said 'Shoo', but shoo it was unable to do, though its wings were perfectly formed, if a bit small.

It was silly really – my concern, I mean – because I'd just slaughtered millions of aphids and not asked one where its mother was. I was about to go indoors when I noticed next-door-but-one's cat padding along the wall. What a dilemma! Now, I'm a bit of an ornithologist in my spare moments, having once, several years ago, mothered a young bird who was the victim of an earthquake. This was not in Camden Town, of course, but up a mountain on an island in Greece. The bird was called Kowalski, after Marlon Brando in *A Streetcar Named Desire*, and I kept him alive for four days in a hurricane. The thing is, nature always knows best, and it's really useless trying to interfere. On the fifth day the bell tolled for Kowalski and he died of overfeeding.

Anyway, I ran indoors, tipped half a ton of nuts and bolts out of an old cardboard box, punched holes in it, fetched bread and water, and was out down the back steps in a jiffy. It was quite a deep box, but when I popped the weak creature inside it grew frightfully cross, flew up and out and waddled back to the geranium pot. At that moment the telephone rang. When I returned the bird had gone and the cat was leaping along the wall with something in its mouth. So I shed a few tears.

At night, with my daughter Jo Jo, I went to the South Bank for *An Evening with Dame Edna*. That's when I cried again, though it was mostly with laughing. The telly people were awfully hospitable. Drinks before the show – lots of them – drinks after the show, and food. They did us proud, as they say, but I was a bit sad we weren't given gladioli to wave. Dame Edna had one, and it sort of went limp when she was singing her song.

Jo Jo was beside herself spotting celebrities. Sir John Mills was across the gangway, but she was far more impressed by the stand-in, Sir Les Patterson, who was sitting next to us. He had egg on his Y-fronts. Behind us were Dr and Mrs Anthony Clare and Derek Hatton and Sam Whatsit and Mr and Miss Ingrams and a Rolling Stone whom she afterwards accosted, and Ringo Starr. Best of all, I met that marvellous actor Geoffrey Palmer and his wife, and they were both lovely.

Dame Edna was in terrific form and her skin was much admired. I think she's on hormones. She was in a red slinky frock to begin with, and then after the interval she changed into a powder-blue number with a swirly bodice and a short skirt run up by her son Kenny, the dress designer. She never stopped making us laugh, great billows and bellows of delight that rolled round the studio and had us shaking in our seats.

Laughter is a marvellous sound. We don't do enough of it. The bit where I cried was when someone asked her if she was enjoying widowhood. I hadn't known Norm had been disconnected and it came as a bit of a shock. Actually, I think it suits her – being Normless, that is. She's gained a new maturity, a quiet poise which is very moving.

We had supper in a tent, though I can't remember how we got there, and I have the distinct impression we were floating down river.

When we first arrived at the South Bank, Jo Jo was a bit inclined to go on about how much people received on the DHSS and how a fraction of the hospitality would have kept a family of four in choccy bickies for weeks, but she soon got into the swing of it, so much so that when it was time to go home I had to pick her up off the floor. The baby-sitter said she fell through the door.

I had the most confusing dreams that night, all about climbing the north face of St Paul's, hand in hand with Dame Edna in a gale-force wind. In the morning when I went down into the backyard, wincing in the sunlight, that little dicky bird was perched in the geranium pot. All's well that ends well.

Footnote. I've had another letter about my treatment of cats. I do feel I've been misunderstood. Mrs Marie Briggs of Hatch End writes that some people will go out of their way to protect animals. She herself is about to go off to the Shetlands to help a lost finch who has apparently been blown off course. I wish someone would do the same for me.

34. Citizen's arrest

I'm not going to go into this one. I like my bank manager, and I daresay it's not his fault that times have changed and that banks are not what they were. Also, I'm solvent, which makes one feel less critical.

I feel rather like Perry Mason at the moment, or Ironside – they may be one and the same – or even Spencer Tracy in *Inherit the Wind*. Perhaps the latter is going a bit far. At any rate, I've become very involved in the law. Let me explain. Two weeks ago the cleaner took my Access card to the hole in the wall and prodded the wrong numbers. Twice, in fact, which resulted in the card being gobbled up. She went into the bank and told them what had happened, and the bank said I could have it back on Tuesday.

I was short with the cleaner, but she said she was in love and distracted, and I did see her point of view. The following afternoon I ran out of the front gate to buy ciggies and stepped into a heap of dog pooh. I was jumping up and down cursing, when my next door neighbour came home and implied I should pull myself together. When I told her why I was leaping about in such a corybantic fashion, she conceded that I had cause and suggested I should have a camera at the ready to snap the offending, defecating animal, perhaps with its proud owner in focus, and then make a citizen's arrest. 'Can't *you* do it?' I said. 'I'll hide behind the bins and give verbal support.'

On the Tuesday I rang the bank – I'm being a bit coy about the name, but it rhymes with Bat Pest – and the child on the other end said they'd cut my card in two.

'Why?' I asked.

'Well,' he piped, 'it's against the law to give your card to another person.'

Now that's a really heavy statement when you think about it, implying ultimate arrest and prosecution. 'What law?' I enquired.

'You signed a contract,' he said. 'You can't give your number to all and sundry.'

Have you ever heard of such uninformed rubbish? When I first got my card, accompanied by that warning on the envelope to memorise and swallow on sight, it took me days to open the flap. Then, once into the swing of things, I gave the secret digits to everyone I knew; some of them, those who don't often wash, have them stamped to this day in faded biro on their wrists. I make free with my numbers out of expediency; it's impossible to get prompt service from the Bat Pest.

Once upon a time, years ago, we had a lovely interior, oak-panelled, and six tellers who had familiar faces. Now, we have twelve stalls, invariably staffed by three, and a wall at the end papered in plastic planks. But let me return to this vexed question of the Law. If I give my Access number, and card, willingly, knowingly, to a hundred people, a thousand people, it is as though I myself am shoving that bit of plastic through the hole in the wall. If Christ, to misquote poor old Richard II 'found truth in all but one, I in twelve thousand none', then that's my bad luck and I take the consequences.

Should my card be stolen and the number be extracted from me by torture, then perhaps I can get recompense. Mind you, it might prove difficult, for I have not forgotten the astonishing case of the missing £150. Several years back I went to the bank to obtain holiday money. I had gone to the counter downstairs, drawn out £150 in fivers and climbed one flight of stairs to the travellers' cheques department. I placed my handbag at my elbow and indulged in a little light-hearted badinage with my bank manager who had left his maximum security wing to wish me *bon voyage*. Seconds later I dipped into my bag to find a pen and discovered that the money had gone. You could have knocked us all down with a feather. I was advised to wait until the end of the day,

He asked for an overdraft! A typical afternoon at the Bat. Nest.

until the accounting had been done, before informing the police.

All the same, spying two policemen outside the bank, I hastened to tell them of the theft; all they did was to pester me for the name of my employer. I had taken out another £150 and, in dumb show, proceeded to demonstrate how difficult it was to nick a bundle of fivers not bound by a lassy band. The sight of the notes almost got me arrested.

A correspondence lasting many months went on between the bank and me. The words 'supposed theft' were used, which can only mean that they thought I hid the money about my person or handed it to an accomplice on the way up. I would have thought that banks were insured against robbery, but apparently not.

Enough of old wounds – back to the citizen's arrest. I waited two days, camera on the hall shelf, before my moment came and a brown dog with a fluffy tail stopped outside the gate and obligingly did its business on the pavement. Unfortunately, there was no sign of an owner, and you can't citizen's-arrest an animal because an arrest is unlawful unless the person arrested knows why it's happening. Also, the dog was very big.

The very next day another animal, smallish this time, performed on the same spot. Accordingly I rushed out and faced its owner who was loitering by the hedge. 'I'm making a citizen's arrest,' I said, and he said, 'It's a nice day for it', and strolled off.

So much for justice. All I've got is some quite nice studies of poohs, which may raise a few eyebrows when they come to be developed. For all I know, such photographs are against the law.

35. String quartets

It's such a loss that there is no longer a difference between the political parties. In my day, members of the Liverpool Labour party were socialists; now they're called militants.

When I was growing up in Formby by the sea I was invited to a concert by an elderly lady whose husband had been a music critic on a Liverpool newspaper. She was obviously educated, marrying a man like that, and what my mother called well-bred – for instance she drank coffee after her meal instead of tea.

I don't remember much about the concert, except that it was performed by a string quartet, but afterwards I was introduced to another elderly lady called Mrs Criddle whose husband was something big in sugar and practically owned Tate and Lyle. Several days later Mrs Criddle asked me to tea. It was a wonderfully dusty house, gloomy and packed with books and sepia photographs of men with staring eyes under peaked caps. When we had tea nobody bothered with saucers and you could drop as many crumbs as you liked because there was a dog called Olga who rushed forward and snaffled them up. The house was full of people who looked like tramps, spoke like teachers and called each other comrade. When anyone wanted to say anything really important – like the 'Bevin boy' who was recuperating from a fall of coal – Mr Criddle banged a gong and asked us to 'lend a sympathetic ear'. Even Olga sat still and listened.

I went to the Criddles every week for almost a year, and I was lent books to read, and taken to the Walker Art Gallery to look at pictures. Once we went to the Unity Theatre to see a play called *The Man with a Plan* which was very boring. It wasn't enough, Mr Criddle said, to fight for socialism, one must also strive for the sort of enlightenment which could only be achieved through an appreciation of beauty. My father agreed with him in essence if not in fact. He had no doubt that art was a good thing, though personally it didn't agree with him. He was more concerned about the fight for socialism, and had not recovered from the 1936 Labour Party Conference which cast grave doubts on whether any Englishman over the age of forty would ever live to see a Labour government in power again.

I must say, politics seemed more fun in those days. What discord the subject created within the family circle! How I loved to sit at the tea-table and listen to my grandfather and father, both fully paid-up members of the ruling classes when it came to women, spitting at one another, tossing names like fireworks over the cups and saucers – Ramsay McDonald, the Red Dean, Stalin, Bevin and Bevan, that appeaser Chamberlain, that swine Churchill.

What excitement it caused when my grandad, jamming on his homburg hat, left the house vowing never to set foot over the welcome mat again, my grandmother scurrying along in his wake with a humbug in her cheek. What about the sardine can flung at the kitchen window, its broken glass later described as delayed war damage, or the lawn mower that was heaved bodily over next door's fence during an argument about the Russian Front? Not to mention all those fine phrases ... 'A policy of accommodation towards the needs of capitalism will be the death of socialism' ... 'A Labour movement which ceases to fight the ruling classes ceases to exist'.

I was reminded of those halcyon days last week when I went to a party at Toynbee Hall to celebrate the publication of W. J. Fishman's new book, *East End 1888* – a tragic chronicle of poverty, exploitation, murder and misery. Reading its pages, its account of universal degradation, of individual suffering, one is hard put to believe in the love of God. Toynbee Hall is in Commercial Street, set back from the road within a garden of grass and rambler roses. Its purpose, in the beginning, was to provide a meeting place, a club house for those whose interest in the poor leapt beyond the belly to the mind. With Ruskin and Mr Criddle, its members held that 'life without industry is guilt, life without art is brutality'. With admirable zeal they sought to mingle with the poor, break down class barriers and encourage 'that healthy instinct for art which exists within the sons of labour'. One could knock the idea as patronising and idealistic, but in many cases it bore fruit. Of course, the telly hadn't been invented then, and the welfare state was in private hands.

It was a good party and there was a lot of excellent chat about socialism in the old days, football hooliganism and Jack the Ripper. Some of us wondered whether a gentle fostering of the arts by football clubs, poetry readings by centre forwards at half time, a snatch or two from the *Nuns' Chorus* before kick-off, would have a calming effect. Others, myself included, felt that harsher sentences for offenders, involving compulsory attendance at concerts and modern art exhibitions, would prove to be more of a deterrent. There's nothing like a string quartet to make one see the error of one's ways.

36. The gall of it

Had I come home on my own I would have required smelling salts. Brian, our present speaking-clock, is lovely. He put a message on my answering machine on my birthday.

Something happened yesterday; I went to visit a friend recovering from an operation for gall-stones. What *is* it about hospitals that makes one feel queasy the moment one passes through the portals? It was a private hospital off Marylebone Road and exceedingly clean and casual, but once in the lift I immediately came down with stomach ache. So bad was it that, on finding my friend sitting up in a chair with drips dangling from him, I pinched his bed and lay down.

After a bit he began to grumble that he was uncomfortable and demanded his bed back, and it was terribly difficult getting him out of the chair. He was clad in a little blue shortie nightie that left nothing to the imagination and he kept becoming entangled in his life-support cables. His language was dreadful. Then the bed was too low and had to be cranked upward, only I wound too quickly and it jack-knifed him. When he'd forgiven me we had a riveting discussion about gall ducts and the building up of bile, and then I remembered his present, which was a book called *Hitler's Table Talk*, and he said how thoughtful I was and how it was just what he needed, considering his condition. Then we debated whether he ought to have a cigarette and decided against it in case he got a fit of coughing and blew off his drips. As a sort of concession I exhaled my smoke in his direction. Before I left he gave me his gall-stone for my museum collection.

I don't put just any old thing in my museum. Among many less interesting items I have a piece of Herod's Temple, my mother's teeth, a diary for 1946 which has only one entry

– for the 21st of January ('The sky interests me. Is God there?/My first banana. Tastes like milky cheese') and a sock, discarded in the lounge of the Tel Aviv Hilton, belonging to Melvyn Bragg.

As I was busy that afternoon I left the gall-stone in its plastic pill box on the kitchen table, and it was still there in the evening when I went out to a dinner party. I know that, because beside it was my newly-acquired Access card – you may remember that only two weeks ago the original was shredded by mistake – a photograph of Brian the speaking clock, and half a packet of cigarettes.

It was a smashing dinner party. The guest of honour couldn't come at the last minute, and we'd all waited for him for so long that we were more than lit up by the time we sat down to eat. The food was glorious – I don't hold with food in general, but this was proper fodder, tatties and mint and beef with fat – and the conversation was salacious and gossipy and much hingeing on the those dear, bad, gone days when we all felt, coming from the North, the suburbs, the Commonwealth, that London belonged to us. There was also another conversation about the ills of the world: wars, male violence, etc, being due to men not being able to spill their seed without guilt. I wish I had been in a state to record this in more detail. At any rate, I rolled home at about one o'clock, escorted by two friends, aimed my key unsteadily at the lock, and found the door already open. There was furry mud on the carpet, and the cat was sitting underneath the water buffalo. The lock was on the floor mixed with some splinters of door jamb.

The first priority was ciggies, seeing the ones on the table had been nicked. So had the video machine, the Access card and £10 worth of two-pence coins kept in an old cash register beneath the sewing machine. The fortunate thing was that Becca downstairs had heard footsteps, knew I was out, and had rung me up. My machine speaks out loud, and I think this scared off the intruders.

A very nice policeman came round in the middle of the night. He said nothing about Eric (the buffalo) as he squeezed up the hall, though his expression spoke volumes, and he took down the particulars jolly smartly. He also told us to ring Access there and then, and gave us numbers of all-night locksmiths. He said his hat was very heavy. We said the badges looked a bit tinny, not genuine, and he said – more or less – beggar the badges, it's a crash helmet.

Thinking about it now, days later, it seems to me that the experience sums up the age we live in. Some youths (no self-respecting, mature burglar would take two-pence pieces) smashed in the front door of a house bought for £8,000 and now valued at more than a quarter of a million, to steal a hired video and a plastic card in order, according to the police, to raise money for drugs. They were disturbed by a telephone call that spoke into thin air. The occupier of the house, divorced, subsequently a single parent, was out, pontificating under the influence of another, more acceptable drug, upon a past which has become more real than the present. The figure of the law came round in a hat designed to prevent his skull being crushed. On the table stood a specimen swirling in bile, not considered to be worth pinching, a geological lodestone of the human condition, removed by the private sector at the cost of thousands.

For the life of me, I can't think who's more to be pitied .... me or them.

37. Huge interest

I can remember very little of all this apart from buying the crucifix, a purchase which later inspired me to carry home half a ton of plaster and sculpt on chicken wire the figure of the playwright, James Barrie. He was intended to stand on his own two feet, but a gradual sagging at the knees has required him to be seated. In spite of his homburg hat he looks every inch a lost boy.

One way and another, last week was something of a hotch-potch. As I am under the impression that I lead a quiet life and very rarely go out, I find it astonishing how many things I apparently fitted in. I see in my diary that I was driven by the dashing Gilbert to the North East London Polytechnic to assist in choosing a headmaster for the school of Independent Studies. This experience along the corridors of power was marred only by the realisation that the losing candidates had to be told to their faces that they'd been passed over. At this point I tried to hide behind the curtains and was sternly rebuked for cowardice by the Rector. I did think I could wear my Doctorate of Letters gown, but no such luck. I've had this splendid garment for three years now and have had no opportunity of showing it to a larger public, and sadly it has been attacked by moths, as has its owner.

The following day I travelled up to Liverpool to attend a dinner held by the Independent Broadcasting Authority, a splendid occasion marked by two very good after-dinner speeches, one by Lord Thomson and the other by the Recorder of Liverpool. In the bar afterwards – Heavens, how everyone drinks these days – I had a spirited discussion with two lads called John and Chris, to whom I explained that soon the BBC as we all know it will no longer exist. They seemed quite interested, but turned out to be from the Nat West rather than the IBA.

Travelling home on Inter City – one hour late and a detour round Birmingham – we were constantly bombarded with messages and instructions from a gregarious guard who was hell-bent on describing both the scenery outside the window and the fillings in the sandwiches in the refreshment coach. 'Do not leave the train without your luggage,' he bade us, as we stopped in a field among grazing cows.

The next day I received through the post the details of my remortgage arrangements from the Abbey National. On a loan of £6,000 I pay back – in 15 years – £13,000. Now, grateful as I am for the loan, I find it extraordinary that it should be such a huge sum. I can't think why I didn't know about these things before. It has only just occurred to me that the interest paid by the bank for keeping one's money in a deposit account is not down to kindness – a sort of bonus for being thrifty – but because they've been lending it to all and sundry for years, and no doubt charging *them* hefty interest. I mean, protest as one likes against usury and such things, none of us is innocent. What I want to know is, who's lent me the six thousand, and do they know what I want it for?

I was full of this vexing problem on Sunday when I went to a party to celebrate the recovery of a friend from a nasty stroke. Everyone sympathised with me and did sums on the backs of envelopes, but I was assured that it was perfectly above board and normal practice. In the middle of all this I began to feel strange, sort of light-headed, which had nothing to do with the champagne. The following morning, the feeling grew stronger. I put it down to brain fatigue from all that travelling and choosing heads of department, not to mention adding up interest rates.

In the afternoon I wandered through Dingwall's Market and saw a very large crucifix complete with a bleeding-heart Jesus, and snapped it up. Carrying it home down the centre of the street – at the weekend the pavements of Camden Town are too crowded to walk on – I began to hear voices, drum beats, snatches of song. To my left I saw a St John

Ambulance with a cheery soul waving me on encouragingly, and to the right a stout lady running alongside with a tray of coke tins. The drums increased in volume. Turning round, and it wasn't easy with Jesus in my arms, I was flustered to see I was at the head of a vast procession carrying banners. I dropped out and hid behind the gates of the Greek church, and the people flowed past me, heading for Hyde Park and a rally in protest against the imprisonment of Nelson Mandela. Still, it was an awkward moment; I could well have led them straight back to my own modest home.

On the Monday I was even worse – head-wise, I mean – I was now floating a lot when I was vertical, and hallucinating when I was horizontal. I knew that at noon Robert from *Woman's Journal* was coming with a ton of bubbles to photograph me in the bath – we writers are never idle – and it was quite likely I should drown. They would all be so busy setting up lights and re-arranging the bubbles that they wouldn't notice me going under for the third time. So I cancelled and retired to bed, where I sit at this moment with my fountain pen leaking all over the sheets.

I had a very odd dream a few moments ago – I was in my gown entering Jerusalem and Nelson Mandela was up a tree at the side of the road, waving. I waved back and, just as I passed, he shouted out, '178 payments at £75.25p a week for fifteen years.' Then I woke up, thinking that by then the BBC as we know it will have ceased to exist. Come to that, at the rate I'm going, so will I.

38. Guilty gals

I became a Catholic in Scotland, while I was a member of the Dundee Repertory Theatre Company. In England, in those days, turning to Rome required parental consent. I had looked forward to passionate arguments, mainly to do with sexual matters, while being instructed by one of the nuns. Mine was ninety and had entered the convent at the age of twelve.

There's a new phenomenon abroad, that of the touting driver who roams the kerbs of the West End asking pedestrians if they require a cab. It doesn't help that these hopeful chaps are invariably sinister of appearance. Three times the other night I was approached by gentlemen all bearing a striking resemblance to Oliver Reed as Bill Sykes and offered a lift home. On each occasion I patted them nervously on the arm and said: 'No thanks, nothing personal, but I don't know you from Adam.' Daft really, because five minutes later I jumped into a taxi without a qualm. It was a lovely night, warm and breezy, with a great gong of a moon riding the clouds above the pizza palace in Cambridge Circus. I felt quite safe walking the streets, in spite of the jostling crowds and the youths on bicycles doing a *Tour de France* along the pavements.

When I first came to London, in the fifties, I thought the West End was the wickedest place on earth. I wore my heart in my boots just walking into Lyons Corner House, and no wonder, because someone slipped a Mickey Finn – you don't hear of them any more – into my cup of coffee and two hours later knocked a tooth out of my jaw. I went to the police, which was a mistake, because I was under age and they wanted to contact my parents, so I gave a false name and ran out. I know I went to the Brompton Oratory to find a priest, but they were all having supper, so I went to a dentist instead, although that was the following day.

38. *Guilty gals*

Anyway, I was sauntering along the streets at midnight the other evening because I'd just had a splendid supper in the company of one chap and six 'gals'. The chap was none other than John Walsh, literary editor of this very newspaper, who is writing a book on the lasting effects of Catholic childhoods. We girls, loosely speaking, were there to pass on our experiences and emotions. Actually, my being there was a bit of a cheat, in that I was brought up a Protestant and only began to swivel towards Rome in adolescence, a time at which everyone else at the table, bar one, appeared to have turned in precisely the opposite direction. I say 'bar one', because Karen had gone over the top and been a nun for seven years. It was she who explained to me, and I wasn't the only one to be knocked down by a feather, that it was the Virgin Mary who was the Immaculate Conception, not Jesus, who was the Virgin Birth. I was instructed into the church by a very elderly nun in Dundee and she certainly never mentioned Mary's mother.

It was a spirited evening. Young Walsh kept firing profound questions ... What about hell? ... What about Heaven? ... What of sex? We all had very strong notions about the first and last subject, but no opinions at all on Heaven. God knows what the waiter made of it. One moment we were deliberating over sins of omission and the next we were discussing whether it was an occasional sin to cut nuns' knickers off at the knee in the interests of hygiene on the Northern Line. As for Guilt, we all had that, especially Claire and Maggie, though we came to the conclusion that most of it had to do with being female and beggar all to do with religion. Young Walsh's guilt centred a lot on being behind bicycle sheds, whereas the rest of us could feel guilty anywhere. Karen said that she had known a nun who had taken to her bed for three days because the convent cat had gone missing. This was on the way to being a sin, as all love rightly belonged to God.

I'm not sure that people are capable of believing with the same intensity any more. Too many rules have been changed. I well remember, some years back, the disillusionment felt by a Catholic woman who was told by her priest that she must forgive her husband for running off with the next door neighbour. 'All my life,' she said, 'I've been taught that hell fire awaits the adulterer, and overnight I'm expected to condone it with forgiveness.' It didn't help that the following year the priest ran off with the wife of Cairo Joe who kept a chandler's shop in Myrtle Street.

Footnote. I received last week a lovely letter from 'Fred' of NW5. I think it's worth quoting at length ... 'There's an undercurrent in your *Evening Standard* pieces of the last few weeks that gives me the heeby-jeebies. In order to cheer you up I have been finding purely scientific facts about Beryls – this stone is brought out of India; it is like water and even more like crystal. When the sun shines the royal Beryl throws back fire into the sun's face; it loves all matrimony and contains all the sorrows of the spleen, but, if you have a Beryl set in your ring, put a bit of savin behind your left knee and you will never wax wroth with the woman you wedded. Albertus Magnus in his book of minerals reports that if this stone is good and genuine it cannot abide sexual intercourse. Spectacles were invented in the thirteenth century, and the oldest vernacular word for them is Brille – the German for Beryl. I hope that any of this that is news to you is cheering. Yours, Fred.'

39. Exchanging words

I had a long talk with Molly, but for the life of me I can't remember why she had to be treated so gently. It's odd, because whatever it was sparked off the entire article.

Last weekend I had a most vexatious argument about politics and the meaning of words, two stimulating topics which I feel sure you will be interested in. Just to set the picture, the earlier part of the day had been spent at a 'brunch' party of bagels and smoked salmon and malt whisky in NW3. Bagels, I discovered, have nothing to do with dogs, being round bits of bread, sort of twisted; in other words a southerner's version of the Lancashire bap, only with a hole in it. At this brunch we discussed operations of the medical sort, the Third World and suicide. I suspect there's a logical, cheerful link somewhere, in that surgery is painful, inhabitants of the Third World are starving to death and suicide is usually fatal.

I can't say it was an uplifting conversation. Of course, the heat and the bagels may have had something to do with it. I travelled there in a cab with Mr Haycraft, my publisher, who was barefoot with a bow tie – he had a blister on his heel – and Alice Thomas Ellis, or Anna, his wife, who said if he didn't shut up and drop dead she'd go straight home. He, never at a loss for small talk, turned confidentially to the driver and murmured '*Annuimus pariter vetuli notique columbi.*' (For those very few who don't understand, please look at foot of column.) There was a lady doctor from the Third World who was bothered that her mother, Molly, was coming 'down' any moment to join the party. A girl called Jenny and I were urged not to mention 'certain things' when Mum arrived. We could tell the warning was urgent, but we both felt like characters in that episode from *Fawlty Towers* in which Basil is expecting German guests and has been urged not to mention the war.

In the event we waited anxiously, evangelically almost, for the descent of Molly, and during this trying time Anna brought up the suicide of her granddad, Herr Lindholm – perhaps Per Lindholme, seeing he was Scandinavian – in the upstairs room of *The Nook* public house in the Chinese quarter of Liverpool. *The Nook* in my day was run by Eileen, who wore purple, and her son who was called either Worthington or Waterloo. On a Friday night the single boys sat lined up against the wall and the unmarried girls paraded in sarongs for their perusal, with a view to marriage.

Fifty years earlier, Anna's grandpa had taken his family to a hop, returned home and retired to bed. His wife and daughters sat downstairs reliving the evening's triumphs and discussing the dresses, the bubbles in the lemonade, the extraordinary reticence of the Houghton sisters. At some point Dad, heaving himself up from the blankets, shouted out: 'If you women don't get to bed, I'll shoot myself.' And he did. We went to visit the pub ten years ago, and the family name was delicately engraved in the glass of the saloon door. Anna offered to buy it, and clinched the deal, and then a week later some chap put his foot through the door, shattering the glass and the past.

After the party a group of us wandered across the heath and lay on the grass beside the shimmering pond. It was probably shimmering because one's eyeballs were whirring. But it was beautiful; the sun, the weeping trees, the muddy water, the shadows dappling the parched grass.

On the way home I got involved in this political argument with a chap who appeared out of some bushes. I don't remember how it started, but it all appeared to hinge on the word 'conservative'. He said it was obviously to do with conservatories, as in greenhouses. Detaching myself, I rushed home and looked it up in the dictionary. Words are funny things. Did you know that Tory, in Irish, was a bog-trotter, or one who pursued. Later it became a nickname applied to those who opposed the succession of Charles II's brother, Catholic James, Duke of York. In 1837 – I've looked it up – there was a lot of bad feeling against changing Tory to Conservative. It's worthwhile listing the objections of the time. Lord John Russell, a Liberal, wrote: 'I fear it is a mere change of name, a mere alias to persons who do not like to be known under their former designation and who, under the name of Conservatives, mean to be conservative only of every abuse; of everything that is rotten; of everything that is corrupt.' Russell preferred reformers. Luther, he said, was a reformer, whereas Leo X, who opposed the Reformation, was a Conservative. Earlier, Macaulay had described 'conservative' as a new cant word.

Yes, I did look up 'cant', and out of a long list picked out: 'To whine like a beggar ... possess a slanting face ... sell by auction.' I was going to look up 'bagel', but by this time my brain hurt.

Footnote. 'We bill and coo together like old familiar doves' (Ovid).

40. Cages

Darling Bertie still has an affinity with monkeys. He often shins up the back of the door and hangs quite comfortably by one arm.

Last week I took my grandchildren to the zoo in Regent's Park. We have all been many times before, but a visit never palls. In order of preference, the gift shop is favourite, then the monkeys, followed by the tigers and the alligators. Charlie had his camera with him and took many pleasing shots of the bottom of cages and the tops of trees ... and one of me with my head stuck in a cardboard cut-out of a gorilla. Strange how that one came out properly in focus.

The children's zoo was not a success. There were so many little hands patting the rabbits that the poor things had gone flat as ironing boards. Trying in vain to get a stroke of the guinea pigs, a flaxen-haired tot burst into tears. 'Forget it,' cried her Dad, obviously a keen nature lover, 'it's only an overblown mouse.'

Darling Bertie fell over and hurt his knee but refused to be kissed. He said it was all right as he had done a bit of swearing and that made it better.

'You swore?' I asked, shocked at such profanity in a young child. 'What word did you use?'

'I do it in my head,' he said, 'so I wasn't listening.'

He was wearing an over-large safari hat made of leather and what we call his Chariot of Fire shorts, and when we went to look at the tigers he had only to put his diminutive nose to the wire for every animal in sight to lope towards him. It was quite amazing. Charlie and I tried borrowing the hat but it didn't work. If Bertie's effect on the tigers had been interesting, his presence outside the various monkey enclosures was downright awe-inspiring. At one point he and a

Bertie striking up a rapport at the zoo.

chimpanzee stood mouth to mouth – the glass between – for at least five minutes, gazing cross-eyed and besotted at one another. I still can't make it out. I suppose they could have mistaken him for a hunter, bearing in mind the hat, but surely anyone could see he was an exceptionally small big white hunter, and he was carrying his pink juice-cup.

And then something happened which made me realise how attitudes have changed in the last decade. Two small girls of about eight years of age approached the gorilla enclosure where a solitary female was glowering through the wire. 'Yuk,' cried the girls, contorting their faces in disgust, at which an elderly lady cuffed one of them mildly over the head and told them not to be rude. I suppose it's television that has altered the way in which we perceive animals. And yet, contrary to popular belief, we have often condemned cruelty.

More than a hundred years ago a Madame Fontaine was pilloried in the press for riding in her birthday suit upon a heifer attached to a balloon drifting across London. In her defence she said, more or less, that she was only trying to earn an honest few bob depicting an air-borne Lady Godiva. 'What the public wants,' she is reported to have said, 'is spectacle. I was fulfilling a need.' Everybody was sorry for the heifer, but nobody seemed to have any pity for the aeronautical Madame Fontaine. But then she was only a woman, whereas the heifer was an animal.

Which reminds me of something that also happened last week, although on this occasion I was not present and can only rely on hearsay. In an odd sort of way it has to do with zoos and heifers, cruelty to an endangered species, big white hunters and 'Yuk'.

Let me set the scene. My eldest daughter – never to be confused with the youngest who has been known to go off like a hand-grenade at the merest sniff of a glass of sparkling Vimto – went out for the evening with the cleaner. The first part of the outing was spent at an edifying art show, the second at the *Lamb and Flag* public house in Covent Garden. On entering, the cleaner wanted to go to the loo. She passed a bald gentleman whose pate she gently patted on her journey to the convenience. Her response to his sweet baldness was no more suggestive than all those kiddies ironing the rabbits, and certainly less explicit than the bum-pinching that goes on in an average female's trek to the lav in any pub any night of the week. My daughter ordered drinks and was told that while she could have one, the cleaner definitely couldn't. Neither of them argued, or so they said, and they went over the road to another pub, were served and carried their drinks back to the original hostelry, though they stayed outside. The night wore on. Towards closing time (and by now the entire male population of the *Lamb and Flag* were legless, singing rugby songs and generally disporting themselves) my daughter confronted the barman and asked for an explanation of his barring of the cleaner.

He was quite a nice bloke. He agreed she hadn't been offensive – not totally – and the man with the bald head hadn't objected to her attentions ... but something bothered him. What it was, he couldn't put a name to. My daughter promptly helped him. 'Sexist,' she said. 'You don't like us to get out of our cages.' I don't think it does any good to delve into the barman's mind. He doesn't know what he was on about. Like Bertie, he was doing it in his head and wasn't listening.

41. Pudding

James Barrie was inspired by Jesus. In order to make him I first fashioned a kind of rough crucifix out of wood and then ripped up old sheets (some not so old) to wrap round and round the cross to pad out the shape before slapping wet plaster all over the sheeting. The particular plaster I used dries very quickly. In the end I had to break James Barrie's legs in order to sit him down. He was too big standing up. He did become seated, but not before half the plaster had fallen off, including some of his trousers. If the plaster wasn't so crumbly and wouldn't make so much mess, I might by this time have carted him out to the bins. As it is, we'll both have to be carried out together.

Pudding was Pudding and had her own cross to bear.

Driving through London on a Sunday is very interesting because you can see the houses properly. Have you noticed that when the streets are choked with traffic one is too bad-tempered to look at things? Mind you, the hideous aspect of the Elephant and Castle could strike one blind.

I was on my way to Peckham Rye to lunch with friends in their newly-bought flat, and very posh it was too, not to say clean. They had all the right equipment – forks, knives, chairs, most of which I was without until fifteen years ago – and after lunch we sang songs round the piano in the hall. I came away very impressed. At their age I was renting a thirty-shilling-a-week house of the same size with an outside loo, and the enormous price they had paid for their accommodation only registered when I was halfway home. I grew quite hysterical as we sped in a cab towards the north, thinking of games of Monopoly – £60 for the Old Kent Road, if I'm not mistaken, and only a couple of hundred more for Bond Street.

It put a new complexion on every run-down building from south of the river to Gray's Inn Road, each one, in spite of peeling stucco and leaking roof, a potential goldmine. It's a puzzle to me how this has come about, although I do realise it has something to do with supply and demand. I tried to interest the cab driver in the phenomenon, but he said, somewhat mysteriously, that it was 'out of his hands'. I took this to mean he was in no position to join in either the buying or the selling spree, but it turned out that he had expectations of inheriting a 'tidy stone house' in Lanarkshire the moment his mother passed on, which was any moment now. This information increased my hysteria, because I suddenly remembered I had left a close relation dying on a pile of newspapers in the bathroom, and a life-size plaster sculpture of the Scottish playwright James Barrie spread-eagled on the bedroom floor. The relation, my twenty-year-old cat Pudding, fell ill on Friday. Mr Barrie, face down, began to sweat on Saturday. I loosened the scrim – a technical term for bandages dipped in plaster – wound about Barrie's buttocks, but he still seemed uncomfortable.

I must say I was astonished at the response of my children to Pudding's imminent demise. Their concern, seeing they had studiously ignored her once her kittenish days were over, took me by surprise. My youngest daughter gloomily pronounced it to be the end of an era. Once Pudding went, I was sure to follow. She said we were very alike, backbone and ribs showing, unsteady on our feet, hair falling out, sudden bursts of irritability. 'Take her to the vet,' my son ordered – a man who last noticed the cat when he was ten years old, and then only because he fell over it. I argued that, at twenty, Pudding didn't need euthanasia; that, on the contrary, she had a right to slip into the dark with what remained of her feline senses. 'Let her go with dignity,' I cried. 'Just you wait,' said my youngest. 'Think how you'll feel when we plonk you on the *Sunday Telegraph* on the floor beside the lav.' None of them showed the slightest interest in the strangely perspiring James Barrie.

When I returned from Peckham Rye, Pudding appeared

more lively; she had piddled under the bath. I sang to her for a bit; first, *How Much is that Doggie in the Window?* and then *Where Have all the Flowers Gone?*. The latter went down best. She purred appreciatively, though the cleaner informs me that cats always purr when they are about to die. We've become very close, Pudding and I, in the last twenty-four hours. It's true to say that her value, emotionally speaking, in spite of her balding, emaciated frame, has increased three-fold now that she may be taken from us. She wasn't a very adequate mother, but then who is? She walked away from her first litter and we didn't find the mummified corpses in the upstairs wardrobe until four years later. She ate two of the next lot, and she only licked her final family into life because I stayed with her under the bed and sang *Tulips from Amsterdam*. We kept one of her sons, Gerald Duckworth, and he's brain-damaged on account of the times she's swiped him off the windowsill two floors up. But, damn it all, even if she was neither a good mouser nor a good mother, even if we took no notice of her, she was still a mewing party to all our small triumphs and disasters. She was there when Dad left home for the Commonwealth, when Boy took a hammer to detonators in the front garden, when Grandma came to visit. She gazed through the window at me while I wrote fourteen books, and she watched, tail twitching, as one by one the children left home. She did her business in the back yard beside a two-foot-high mountain ash that now, in stormy winter, rakes its branches against the topmost windows of a four-storey house.

Footnote. At the time of writing, Pudding is still with us. I've just been upstairs to look at James Barrie, and thought him a cold fish. I could have asked, until the cows came home, where all the young men had gone, and he wouldn't have said a word.

42. Big adventure

We never saw Pudding again. Sometime, when I have the energy, I shall make a plaster replica and place her at James Barrie's feet.

I was going to tell you about the peaceful end of my cat, Pudding, whose illness I mentioned last week, but fate has played an unkind card. There she was, if you remember, purring away like a small steam engine, and we were already engaged in planning the funeral. Bertie was practising 'There's a friend for little children above the bright blue sky', and I was ringing up taxidermists in the Yellow Pages. Not that I got anywhere. There is a firm close by who apparently stuffed Guy, the gorilla, when he passed on, but when I telephoned they said they didn't do cats and dogs. It seems owners are too fussy about the results; they want 'life-like' cadavers. When I said that this particular owner wasn't at all fussy, and that a dead-like animal was perfectly in order, they said it still wasn't worth it; cats are too small. It does make one wonder what people in NW1 keep in the way of pets.

Anyway, at some point during Tuesday of last week I was persuaded to call a vet. What a mistake. First, I had a terrible row with a receptionist, who haughtily said her medical man was far too busy to make a house call. Indeed, she implied that such a request was wildly impertinent and announced vindictively that it would cost me £45. 'Is that all?' I retorted, quick as a flash, though I was reeling with shock. At the speed of light – I'm convinced he was parked on the corner plugged into his car telephone – the vet arrived, plus girl assistant. There was a slight loss of confidence on their part as they came through the door, although it was only later that I realised this might have had something to do with the sight of Eric, the water buffalo, charging, stuffed, up the hall.

Faced with the more diminutive Pudding, the vet said she had renal failure, also a growth, and then pulled out a hypodermic needle. I've often noticed that television heroes bear no comparison to people in real life. He was nothing like Siegfried in *All Creatures Great and Small.* He didn't say, 'Oh, my dear, be brave', as Robert Hardy would have done. Before you could say boo, he just jabbed her. As he left he gave me some pills which I was supposed to give her every third day. And as I accompanied the boy-vet to the front door, Pudding shot out of the back. We haven't seen her since. Oh, yes, we've looked for her everywhere, but it's nine days now and I don't think there's much hope.

In the meantime, I've been busying myself with my plaster of Paris statue of the playwright James Barrie and, though I hate to admit it, I've gone about as far as a mere woman can go in her endeavours to produce the real man. In other words, I'm giving up. He's turned out to be something of a disappointment. I have invited various critics to view him in an unfinished state – fortunately none of them of the calibre of Brian Sewell – and the response has not been encouraging. The general opinion is that he resembles one of the undead. I think this may have something to do with the material from which he is fashioned. Plaster is rather a crude medium. It falls off a lot. I started with chicken wire, to bolster him up, and then I covered him with bandages dipped in plaster. Then I put underpants on him, and I was going to put real trousers on top. The thing is, every time I pick him up and sit him in a chair pieces of his drawers break off. This can be disconcerting. Also, possibly due to a lack of backbone, he seems incredibly limp. Even his face, complete with a moustache made from cuttings from the yard brush, lacks firmness. He looks outraged, as if he smells something nasty in the woodshed. And I can't get his galoshes on. Well, I can, but his feet have dissolved in the process.

I did go to the Tate on Saturday to view the Picasso exhibition and pick up a few hints, but I can't say it was a help. All Picasso's women have very large bosoms, not always in the right place, and the Henry Moores on the lower floor were full of holes, which is precisely what I've achieved with my James Barrie, and I don't like them. I'm still fond of James. He, in case you don't know, is the man who wrote *Peter Pan,* all about lost boys and Nana, the dog. He also wrote that immortal optimistic line, spoken by Peter when marooned on a rock in the lagoon of Never-Never Land: 'To die will be an awfully big adventure.'

I've just thought that Pudding could well be in next door's garden pond, face down among the lilies. I shall go down soon and have a look. I just feel uneasy. I blame the vet, but the children said I trod on Pudding's tail as I showed the vet to the door. Lost boys or lost cats, it's all the same. There's always guilt.

43. Filthy lucre

The Tatler had the inane idea that it would be fun to commission writers to invent new endings for various novels. I can't remember what I put, but it still rankles that something like three years went by before I was paid.

Have you noticed how difficult it is these days to get a straight answer to a fairly normal question? You'd think it would be simple, in an age hell-bent on computers and Gallup polls and filing systems, to find out the phone number of the managing director of British Telecom; where to stuff a cat; how to buy a greenhouse 6ft by 4ft, or why a particular brand of tablets which used to clear your sinuses – but also induced sleep – has been replaced in favour of a new, less effective formula. Yes, I realise the managing director of BT is far too important a man for his phone number, let alone his name, to be known by his employees, and yes, perhaps far too many people dozed off at the wheels of cars after a quick fix of sinus-clearer, but why is such information so secret?

I mention this because last week I was foolish enough to cross swords with my friendly neighbourhood bank over yet another act of inefficiency on their part. My query, to be fair, seeing that I kept asking why they were so stupid, was hardly likely to elicit a straight answer, but afterwards I went on a fact-finding mission. In other words, what does a socialist do with surplus money? This vexing question arose because I was in the middle of rewriting the end paragraph of *Lady Chatterley's Lover* for *Tatler* magazine, when the disagreement with the bank occurred – but more of Lady C later.

The bank disturbance was over a proposed standing order to my daughter; they sent me a form asking how long I had known her. Following the resulting lively exchange, I rang directory inquiries and asked for the phone number of the head office of another bank. A child, of course, was on the other end. My question where my money would go if I lodged it with them was met with resounding silence. I was passed, as they say, from hand to hand. I am a socialist, I announced. I am anxious that my money will not be lent to the War Office, South Africa, Camden Council, the National Gallery or any airline that bans smoking. Can you reassure me?

You realise that I had, momentarily, a vague aspiration towards cleanliness – the curse of the puritanical classes – a desire to rise above money. These vague, absurd aims are the natural outcome of possessing a product, i.e. filthy lucre, which though desirable at the time, produces, in the end, nothing but guilt. Like a landslide, a lump of money can bring down a mountain; a smaller amount can just as easily bounce into a crevice and be lost forever. I was given so little satisfaction – your money is quite safe/have you a special reserve account?/we don't know a bank called the National Gallery/smoking is not a good thing – that I resolved there and then to have done with banks altogether.

I was all set to go off with a carrier bag and close my account when the cleaner warned me that I wouldn't get away with it. I'd have to give them notice. According to her, my money was probably at that moment on its way to Hongkong to help someone buy a bit of jungle in which to grow lettuces and avocados for the home market. I was so incensed – until I was 35 I'd never set eyes on an avocado, believing it to be some sort of ant-eater – that I threw my carrier bag into the bin and marched back upstairs to the laboratory to finish off *Lady Chatterley*. It was all D.H. Lawrence's fault in the first place, because the last few pages of his book are a fair old comment on the nastiness of money 'if only we were educated to live, instead of to earn and to spend. If men would wear scarlet trousers, they wouldn't think so much of money; they could dance and hop and skip ... they ought to learn to be naked and handsome and dance the old group dances and carve the stools they sit on and embroider the old emblems.'

I must say he knew what he was talking about, even if he did go on a bit about his bowels turning to water and how lovely his John Thomas looked in the moonlight. When I've got a spare moment I'm off to the bank to persuade them all into red drawers. I'm not sure they'll take to stool carving ... but one has to begin somewhere.

44. Grandchildren

We shall have to wait some time before we learn, if ever we do, what wisdom Mrs Thatcher passed on to her grandson.

Some weeks ago, when it was announced that Mark Thatcher and his wife were on their way to making Mrs T a grandmother, I was asked to write an article on the joys of grandchildren. I expect my references in this column to Charlie and Darling Bertie had something to do with it. So I wrote what I thought was rather a pithy little piece and was astonished a few days later to receive a somewhat abrasive letter from four grandmothers.

'We have read your remarks and we must say they are utter rubbish. It is very thoughtless of you to collect toy guns and to play *Hawaii Five-O* with your little grandsons. It is also extremely stupid of you to tell them about pollution, Auschwitz, the First World War and Hitler. No doubt there are many thoughtless people like you in this world, and no doubt this is one of the reasons why there is so much hooliganism and vandalism about.'

Now, I've no interest in defending myself and you'll have to take my word for it that when I tell the children what the Germans did to the Jews I leave out gas ovens and lamp shades. Nor do I linger on the thousands killed in one bright morning on the Somme. However, when it comes to Hitler I do try and explode the myth that an evil human being springs ready-formed from the womb. After all, this could give my grandsons nightmares on their own account. What I do try to explain, albeit ineptly, is that goodness, like badness, is fostered or abandoned through the connivance or example of other people.

Anyway, the letter set me thinking as to what pearls of wisdom my own grandmother passed in my direction, and

I haven't come up with very much – certainly nothing to do with good or evil, or at least not spelt out in so many words. She *did* teach me that a piece of bread squashed into a lump made a perfectly good rubber, and I do remember she showed me how to cast on in knitting by using one thumb as a needle. And she cheated at cards without batting an eyelid. Later, when she was quite old and my mother used to take her down town to the Bon Marché for afternoon tea, she used to wait until my mother's back was turned and then pinch the sixpenny tip left for the waitress. Later still, if she went out on her own she made a habit of coming over faint in the vicinity of public houses. She would sort of huddle against a lamp post, pressing a hand to her heart, and when concerned passers-by asked if they could be of assistance she always said: 'A little glass of brandy would do the trick.' We found out about it after she stopped a neighbour of my uncle's by mistake.

My mother didn't care for her. They'd had a dog when they were small, and they were warned that if the animal did harm to my grandfather's garden it would be destroyed. My grandma, according to my mother, pulled up all the tulips and got the dog sent away. This doesn't put her in a very nice light, but then, my grandad doesn't exactly come out of it smelling of roses. My grandmother once told me that at the age of eleven she had worked in a lollipop factory in Knotty Ash. It was the most riveting confidence she ever made: when I told my mother about it she forbade my grandma to come to the house for weeks. She said it was a disgusting thing to tell a young and impressionable child, and she swore that if I breathed a word of it to anyone I wouldn't get my Brownie uniform.

It's a difficult thing, in these days of television, to know what to tell one's grandchildren. If they happen to look up at the six o'clock news they'll glimpse corpses, floods, atrocities, famines and those cone-shaped nuclear missiles that burst like pretty fireworks in the heavens. There is a danger, should they view such horrors, in shielding them from a truthful explanation. All too often they can be left with the idea that it is not *we* who kill, but *it*. Only yesterday I had to tell Bertie that Pudding, the cat, had gone for good. We'd tried saying she'd gone on holiday but he'd been waiting for a postcard. Actually, when I admitted she had probably crawled under a bush to die, he took it quite calmly. He just wanted to know when and if I was likely to do the same thing.

Footnote. I've received a very kind letter from Liz Caxton of Potters Bar, offering to loan me her cat, Custard, while she's away in Belgium for a year. How very kind people are! She writes: 'I know she can't replace Pudding, but she's a very small, very cross tabby of a "certain age".' I can imagine what she's like, Liz, and what a wrench it must be for you to leave her, and it's sweet of you to have thought of me. Regretfully, I'll have to decline. One Pudding was enough. Custard would only be an anti-climax.

45. Ex-mother-in-law

The bullet hole is still visible on the landing ceiling. Though it's been plastered over one can still see the mark. Poor Nora! She threw herself under a train five years later.

The extension at the back of my house is beginning to shift. It contains the bathroom and the bedroom of the flat in the basement. I have taken professional advice and am assured that it will take another fifty years for it to break off into the backyard, but am wondering if I could possibly blame it on the new British Library which is rearing up a few streets away.

All that pile-driving and hammering and bulldozing can't be doing much good to the surrounding acres, and what, I ask myself, will happen to my bathroom when they start building the Channel Tunnel thingy at King's Cross? Will it accelerate the detaching process, and will I be sitting in the tub one fine day in the not too distant future and find myself suddenly drifting through the rose bushes into the back wall?

It's terribly difficult to get compensation for this sort of inconvenience, as I know to my cost – I once attempted it after somebody tried to shoot me on the stairs and the ceiling came down. I mentioned this little incident, in passing, in my column last year, when I referred to a photograph of my in-laws which I found on sale among the gents' underpants in Top Shop. So many of you wrote expressing concern at my difficulties with my mother-in-law that I did mean to elaborate on the subject at a later date. What sort of gun did she use, was the question most often asked, followed by what sort of knife was in the carpet bag? Are you sitting comfortably? Well, I'll begin.

Twenty years ago I was working in a factory in North

London, sticking labels on bottles of wine. I was on shift work, to fit in with the children, and this particular morning I was just putting on my coat, preparatory to setting off down the road, when there was a loud knocking at the door and there on the step stood my mother-in-law. Actually she was my ex-mother-in-law, but that's neither here nor there. She said she'd come to fetch some photographs of her children when young, which she was sure I had stolen from her in 1957. I could tell by the tilt to her hat that she was determined not to leave until she'd got what she came for, and so I went upstairs to hunt out the family album.

The last time I'd set eyes on her was ten years before when she said I'd put a worm in her tea. I came out of the living-room with the photographs and she was standing on the half-landing, taking something out of her handbag. Most old ladies (she was in her seventies) would have been reaching for their peppermints, but not Nora. She aimed, I pushed her arm to one side – such a *High Noon* reaction is only one of the many skills learnt from watching television – and the bullet hit the landing ceiling, bringing it down. In the house at the time was a lovely man called Don, who was decorating the upper landing. He was rather poor, economically speaking, and to save his one pair of trousers he had removed them and was doing the painting wearing nothing but an old mackintosh. He rushed downstairs and put the kettle on while I tried to soothe Nora, who was somewhat irritable – well, it is annoying isn't it, saving up your old age pension to buy a weapon, not to mention the bus ride across London, and then bungling the whole job?

Before the kettle had boiled she ran out of the house and disappeared, so I went off to label my bottles. I told Pauline at work what had happened but she didn't seem surprised, and then half an hour later the police came. Nora had, apparently, stopped a patrol car and confessed to murdering me. Wishful thinking, I suppose. No, I didn't press charges, and she was out in forty-eight hours with a bottle of pills to keep her calm.

She returned months later from what Dame Edna Everage

would call the maximum security wing of an old people's home with a carpet-bag full of highly-coloured jumpers for the children. She said she'd got the wool by getting up in the night and unravelling the other old ladies' knitting. The knife was at the bottom of the bag and when I tentatively referred to it – the children were hiding from grannie under the table – she said it was a shoe horn.

If I'm honest, though it spoils the story, it wasn't a proper gun, more like an air pistol. She said she was aiming for my vocal chords. The point is that when I tried to get the insurance company to pay for a new ceiling they said I wasn't covered. Nor was Don covered for distress and harassment, suffered during interrogation as to why he wasn't wearing trousers.

Why did Nora do it? She said it was because she thought she was me. Years ago she'd left her children and run off to Paris. It had preyed on her mind and she wanted to punish herself. Seems reasonable to me.

Footnote. Dear M.H. Spurling of Dalston. I passed on your kind letter to the cleaner and she's asked me to thank you and hopes you'll understand that she doesn't feel up to meeting you by the down escalator in Top Shop on Saturday. She also says she doesn't think she's of ethnic origin, unless you count grandparents born in Manchester.

46. Relics

Only last week I went to the launch of a television programme which has an item on the old hotel. Inside, careful scraping of the white paint daubed on by British Rail in the fifties has revealed portions of the original decor glittering with gold leaf. What vandalism we went in for after the war!

I live two or three streets away from King's Cross, an area intersected by railway lines and stretches of canal. If one washed the chalk slogans from the walls and harvested the crop of lager cans and plastic bags which bloom in every gutter, it could be used as the location for a film based on a novel by Dickens.

The St Pancras Hotel, a magnificent Gothic folly, towers above a district in which there are two gasometers, a parish church, a bridge, a canal walk and some fine streets lined with decent Victorian houses. In between, of course, there are wastelands, areas of monumental warehouses once used by British Rail, from whose decaying brickwork sprout weeds and shrubs. In summer, to young eyes, it all looks a bit of a mess. At nightfall in winter it comes into its own as the gasometers, the turrets of the hotel and the curve of the massive engine shed stamp their black outlines against the sky. Now, however, the site is going to be redeveloped. Great talk was made last spring of the houses to be built, the landscaping to be done, the improvement to the environment. Oh yes, and there'd be a few office blocks here and there to make the whole thing worth the investment. Since then, British Rail has apparently doubled its operational requirements. There are rumours that they intend to build a low-level Channel Tunnel station on the area occupied by Camley Street nature park, the Scala cinema and the Bravington block. It also appears that the 'few' offices will in fact take up six million out of ten million square feet of gross development. It would be nice if Prince Charles could see the plans and bring some sanity into the madness and greed which rages unchecked under the banner of progress.

Next Wednesday at the St Pancras Hotel there's going to be a remarkable exhibition of what school-children expect of the development. It'll be on for two weeks. The whole idea was dreamed up by Terry Hargreaves and the exhibits I've seen are jolly skilful and inventive. Even if you don't like kiddies' drawings and such, it's worth going just to see inside the hotel. I've been judging the written work and for a time I was a bit worried that Prince Charles was out of step. I kept coming across the opinion that 'old buildings are tatty and keep falling down'. I was relieved when the penny dropped and I realised that this was a reference to tower blocks built twenty years ago.

There are some lovely pieces on school outings to the area: 'First we went to St Pancras station. We first saw the wall and it was half dirty and half clean and it looks like a wedding cake. We guess it is a hundred years old. We saw a tramp weeing.' And how's this for an eight-year-old's view of society and a way to beat the housing problem? 'Great houses are for Posh people. But some great houses are for Old people. Some of the people live in the countryside on the grass and some people live in the streets on the pavement. If I was old and I was poor and I didn't have a house I would stand behind a person who lives there and I would hide in the bedroom.'

Fifteen years ago, when I was about to publish my second novel, *The Dressmaker*, Karl Miller, then editor of *The Listener*, gave me the opportunity to write an article about my background. It was mostly about what my father thought about his city, Liverpool, and about death. Parts of it still seem relevant today:

'Even the dog purchased for the children fulfilled its function. When the children left, the dog lived on. From its jaws came a smell like rotting leaves. But when death came

Where have all the buildings gone?

for you, the illusion was exposed. Though the room be filled with people, you were alone and no one was going with you.

'What remained when the man died, when his furniture and bits of paper had been dispersed, when his blankets had been sent to the bag-wash to be passed on to someone worthy, was the bricks and mortar of his dwelling place, the space he had inhabited.

'Buildings stayed put. They endured. Memories escaped if there were no walls to keep them trapped. You knew where you were with a heap of stones that had been standing long before you were a twinkle in your grandfather's eye.'

Fortunately my father died before he saw all the landmarks of his life torn down: the house he was born in, the madhouse where his Granddad died, the brewery where his father worked, the church hall where as a boy he sang *Lily of Laguna* dressed in knickerbockers, a lace collar tacked to his velvet jacket. He said men died but the stones piled up by the sweat of their labour survived. How wrong he was.

47. September song

Last year I received a letter asking permission for Episode 7 of Coronation Street to be transmitted in Australia. I said yes, but I wanted a tape, and they charged me £200. There I am, almost thirty years ago, holding up a banner in Ken Barlow's kitchen and shouting, 'Ban the Bomb'. It's enough to make you weep.

I've just discovered something extremely exciting. I don't expect anyone will share my enthusiasm, but did you know that 'September Song' was written by Kurt Weill and Maxwell Anderson?

'Oh, it's a long, long time/From May to December/But the days grow short/When you reach September.'

Kurt Weill was the man who wrote things with Brecht, including *The Threepenny Opera*, which has that song 'Mack the Knife', which is really about the Nazis. They collaborated on another opera, *Mahagonny*, and in that there's a song about a silver dollar. I can't remember the words, but the end line is 'I must have money or I will die.' The dying bit has nothing to do with starvation; it's to do with amassing money for its own sake. I had a recording of it on a 78 and I played it over and over on my gramophone when I still lived in the North.

Maxwell Anderson was an American who wrote a play called *Winterset*, all about a boy and girl in love. I saw it thirty years ago at the Royal Court in Liverpool, too long ago to remember much about it, except that the girl clung to a lamp-post, a bit like Lili Marlene, against a backdrop of sky-scrapers in New York or Chicago. Even if I can't remember the plot I do know, deep down, that it was terribly sad and possibly in blank verse.

I mention 'September Song' because this week I went up

to Granada TV in Manchester to take part in a programme called *Face to Face*. Yes, it does follow the format of the earlier John Freeman programme, though I suspect that the interviewer, Anthony H. Wilson, a chap with very blue eyes, is better than Freeman. Perhaps 'better' is the wrong word; he just takes it a step forward. Anthony Burgess is in the same series, and Howard Jacobson, and all I had to do was sit in an armchair and chat about my life. We got to talking about my dad, and the fact that he was an undischarged bankrupt, and then I confided in full flood, that some time before she died my mother confessed to having tried to do away with herself before I was born.

She had pernicious anaemia, which meant that she had to be injected with a hypodermic used on horses, full of raw liver. She also lost her teeth and underwent something called gold treatment. I'm not clear what this entailed. I don't think South Africa came into it. All I know is she often proclaimed, when she placed her dentures at night on the bathroom window sill, that it was my fault that she'd lost her real teeth. I was placed in the hearth – when I was born, that is. I don't mean I spent every night there. Anthony H. Wilson asked what I meant. Well, he's young. I was in the hearth presumably to keep warm while the doctor revived my toothless mother. At which my dad shouted – so my mum told me – 'How much is this all going to cost?' Then Anthony, quick as a silver dollar, asked me what word came to mind when I thought of money, and I said dirty. And then he asked me about my potty training. The things one talks about on telly these days!

The funny thing was that while we were talking about poohs a line from 'September Song' kept going through my brain: 'So I plied her with tears in lieu of pearls.' I can't think why. Aren't human beings complicated. Perhaps my mother was wearing a string of pearls when she retrieved me from the hearth.

We ended the interview talking about my boomerang theory. I haven't fully developed it, but it's to do with winging out from one's background in a sort of arc and then coming back to the same spot in later life. It's an inevitable process. We put it into practice after the interview because the publicity department took me to the *Coronation Street* studio to be photographed with Ken Barlow. I played his girlfriend, very briefly, before he was married, in about the fourth episode. It was just before his mum went under a bus. We had a cuddle for the camera, and I wanted to ask about Alan beating up Rita, but I thought that was cheeky, so I asked instead what had happened to Linda, Elsie Tanner's daughter, and to his brother, the one that played football. He said Linda came back on a visit years ago and that his brother had turned into that chap in *Brookside,* the one who married Heather and died of an overdose in Sefton Park.

Then I came home on the train, and later that night, seated at the piano – one does that sort of thing in NW1 – I tinkled out 'September Song' with one finger. I like the last stanza, I must say: 'When the autumn weather / Turns the leaves to flame / One hasn't got time / For the waiting game.'

Footnote. If the nice lady who wrote that letter about my having had a tragic life reads this, please don't take it to heart. It's only words.

48. Death and the pox

All this goes to prove that none of us is going to rest in peace.

When I was quite young I was obsessed with cemeteries and the dead. I used to wander down to the church on the road to Formby shore and wrench those black-edged cards – In Loving Memory of Dad, Sincerely mourned by Ted, Bert, Reggie, Auntie Flo, baby Bernadette, Mr Dickenson of the Co-op, and officers of the Fire Station – from the crackling floral tributes tossed into a heap against the fence that kept the pine trees from the graveyard. In hindsight I put my own morbid interest in death down to the times I was born in, that Holocaust age in which Jews were fed to the gas ovens. I say 'my own', though I believe that most children find death an absorbing topic. Perhaps it has something to do with the fact that, contrary to popular belief, the young have a strong notion of mortality.

When I got a bit older, I wanted to be a mortuary attendant, and my father, possibly appalled at the prospect of such a dead-end job, tried to steer my ambitions towards medicine. He wanted me to be a doctor, not a nurse, I'll say that for him. Accordingly, he bought me Virtue's *Household Physician* in two volumes from a second-hand bookstall squashed between a fishmongers and a milliners at the covered market in Chapel Street, Southport. I still remember some of the more riveting afflictions.

Singultus – a sudden, jerking spasm of the midriff, occurring every few moments in bad cases, causing the air to be driven out of the lungs with such suddenness as to produce a noise something like the involuntary yelp of a puppy. When it occurs towards the close of this acute and grave disease, it is sometimes a sign that dissolution is at hand.

Idiocy (Causes of) – masturbation, or self-pollution. These persons are pale, jealous, take a joke as an affront, put the worst construction upon the action of friends. They are irritable, peevish and fickle.

Smallpox – the disease begins with languor and lassitude, with shivering, with pains in the head and loins, with restlessness; all too soon it is followed by universal prostration.

Inebriety – the liquor desire is a result of morbid conditions which produce an abnormal thirst that only alcohol appears to satisfy. Degeneration of mind and body is rapid unless hot temperance drinks, coupled with pool and billiard tables and a teaspoon of nitric acid and cinnamon, are administered.

It occurs to me, as I'm sure it does to you, that every one of this multitude of symptoms, including yelping, could be put under the general heading of one-over-the-eight. Be that as it may, the up-to-date medical knowledge I gained from the perusal of such scientific volumes has stood me in good stead ever since, and never more so than in the last few weeks when I have become increasingly worried about the fate of the graveyard of St Matthias's church on the Isle of Dogs.

I think I mentioned this matter in a previous column – something to do with a landlord who turned out to be a landlady. It now appears that someone or other is thinking of removing the bones of 5,000 corpses from the cemetery in order to build a technological centre (whatever that may be) and that it will cost at least £225,000, excluding VAT, to do so, and a further £10,000 to screen the public from such a distressing disinterment. Furthermore, it is believed that building workers will have to be inoculated against smallpox to dig up the bodies. There can't be a word of truth in this; there is nothing so dry, so dead as human dust.

By one of those coincidences of life, only last week I bought a picture book on the subject – all about Jenner, who discovered a vaccine against smallpox. He found a cure because a milkmaid called Sarah with a cow named Blossom came to him with a spot on her hand. I won't tell you how – you'll have to read it for yourself. It's in a children's book, written by Arnold Sanderson and beautifully illustrated by Sue Harrison. Darling Bertie fell in love with Blossom. It's a sobering thought that without that poxy cow we might all be pock-marked for life, and yelping and universally prostrate into the bargain.

Footnote. In response to my article of the week before last, in which I referred to a rambling rose as AIDS-ridden, I have received a letter from Mr James Hunting of John Ruskin Street, who finds my description offensive. I am sorry if he thought my adjective distasteful, but I assure him that I simply meant that my rose was suffering from an immune deficiency syndrome; i.e. it was a prey to every blight. Albeit clumsily, I was pin-pointing a disease, not a group. While it is unacceptable to label Jews as Yids or Blacks as Darkies, I feel Mr Hunting was over-sensitive in his response. Had I said my rambler was gay and afflicted with pestilence, he would have been justified in his complaint. It seems to me that in taking my references to my rotten rambling rose as an attack on homosexuals rather than aphids, he is revealing his own prejudices, not mine.

49. In irons

The replacement wheel-chair will come in very handy. Also the crutches. You can tell how well I've brought up the children, though I'm at a loss to know what to do with the hypodermic needles.

Years ago I bought a Bath chair from Reg's stall in Inverness Street market. It was for my old age. Remembering tottering down the High Street with my Mum – though in her case it was high heels and the weight of her fur coat rather than old age – I was determined not to be a burden on my children. Some weeks after the purchase my friend Pauline wheeled me round the block to visit Wendy and, arriving at the forecourt of Cobden House, knocked loudly on her door. Wendy was out, and how were we to know it was two o'clock in the morning? Irate residents phoned the police. I was all for running like hell, but Pauline wouldn't let me. When the police came she said I'd lost the use of my legs in childhood and how dare they harass us. When they left she laughed so much that I had to heave her into the chair to take her home, and she went straight through the canvas seat.

I was sad about the chair because I had a crush on Ironside, that detective on telly with the strong eyebrows who was paralysed. There was an episode in which he ticked off a blind girl for feeling sorry for herself, to which she retorted, it was all right for him, seeing he was able-bodied; maybe she was deaf as well, because his wheel-chair was always bumping into things. Anyway, he very affectingly told her about his own disability, and by the time he was through you could tell she was going to throw her white stick out of the window. Anyone watching knew this miracle had been achieved through words.

Last week, following that excellent article in the *Evening*

Standard by John Rae, in which he deplored some of the findings of the working group set up to discover the best ways of teaching English in our schools, I was reminded of Ironside because I happened to watch one of those television programmes in which members of the public are involved in *Candid Camera*-type incidents. A young woman, persuaded she was needed as a stand-in for the Princess of Wales, was besieged by a pretend photographer and a policeman anxious to give her a traffic ticket. Her endeavours to explain her dilemma to the police, her frequent injunctions to the photographer – 'F ... off, I'm not Lady Di' – were greeted with gales of laughter by the studio audience. There were many such sketches, in which almost all the participants were tastefully dressed and wondrously coiffed, and yet the sound track was peppered with bleeps to drown the monotonous use of expletives. To a man and woman, everybody concerned displayed such a paucity of language, a distortion of vowels and a reliance on the four-letter word as to render them inarticulate. This inadequacy of speech had nothing to do with dialect, which has often enriched our vocabulary, and everything to do with ignorance and a perpetuation of the class system.

And then, a day or so later, up popped that new commercial against the use of drugs. A group of youths are seen in party mood playing 'pass the parcel' with a hypodermic needle. Shock, horror! Time fugits – it takes but a second on the box – and we see a boy at the bedside of his dying friend. The victim, naturally, is speechless. His visitor, naturally, finds it hard to string two words together. He has pimples as well. 'You only done it once,' he grunts, or words to that effect. 'It's bloody unfair.' It seems to me that this commercial is a cop-out. We all know that young people of today, anxious to express their feelings, are far more likely to employ a verb beginning with F than an adjective prefixed with B. Either we should use naturalistic speech or endeavour to communicate by means of language. I reached this conclusion after a birthday gathering on Sunday when the family gave me some splendidly useful presents – a soda siphon from the thirties in glittering chrome, a set of surgical hypodermic needles possibly needed for large animals, a pair of crutches and a new Bath chair from the First World War.

I was being wheeled into place in the front garden to have my photograph taken when a young man passing by leapt up the path to lend assistance. In doing so he unfortunately trod on my hardy perennials and I jumped out of the chair to remonstrate. 'Blow me,' he cried, though those were not his actual words. 'It's a miracle.' Ironside couldn't have expressed it better.

Footnote. Mr R. Lancing of Blackheath has written to tell me that he once saw me in Boots the Chemist in Kentish Town and that I looked a 'proper mess'. His own wife never goes out without her teeth. Could I not spruce myself up, he urges. I can assure Mr Lancing that I couldn't go out without my teeth if I tried, but I do take his remarks to heart and the cleaner has promised to give me a good going over with the Ewbank before I next set foot out of the door.

50. Benefit of rates

The digging problem seems to have stopped. I suspect the Council has run out of money. Refuse is something else. My bin men are now privatised and come at four o'clock in the morning. It's wiser to put one's bins – and old cookers – in the gutter, rather than leave them in the proper place in front of the rose bed. Privatised bin men aren't gardeners. They like nothing better than to drag black bags across a newly flowering bush.

I've always been quite law-abiding, until now. I did a bit of ticket avoidance on trains in my teens and I once stole a packet of cornflakes left in a telephone box in Hampstead. I dithered before taking it because I was certain I'd be punished and, sure enough, the very next day I lost my purse and my keys on a 24 bus. However, I'm now in revolt, and I'll explain why. I happened to pop round the corner to my newsagent's and slipped on a pile of gunge on the pavement – you know the sort of thing, old cardboard boxes, bits of sodden carpet, old clothes. Unhurt, I picked myself up and tripped over the edge of a wobbly paving stone.

On the return journey I negotiated yet another battered television set flung out by the betting shop, and half a ton of dog mess, and paused to admire the colourful arrangement of meat bones and Coke tins at the base of a tree. On the other side of the road, opposite my front gate, is a large crater with a No Smoking sign poking out of it. The Gas Board dug the hole one Sunday morning three months ago and hasn't been back since. It did leave some nice little lights winking merrily all round, but they got smashed in a matter of days. Four or five trees to the left there's a sofa tipped on end and a piece of car. The gutters from one end of the street to the other are strewn with rotten fruit, old cans, cardboard cups, betting slips, magazines – you name it, we've got it – and we haven't seen a road sweeper for weeks.

Yes, yes, I hear you cry, what's new? Well, I went indoors and paced up and down the hall (not easy with the buffalo standing there) thinking of the rates I pay, which are something in the region of a thousand a year. Then I made a mental list of the services I pay for and wouldn't be without, police, fire brigade, lighting, and the ones I am already doing without, namely street cleansing and maintenance. Actually, I tell a fib about the maintenance. Only this year 'they' came along and dug up all the paving stones and replaced them with ones that didn't fit. Every now and then the Gas Board, the water board and the telephone engineers arrive and dig up one or two to see how their pipes and their cables are getting on. The stones vanish without trace, and many weeks later nasty squares of tar appear instead. If one had the inclination one could play dominoes in our street.

After a good moan to myself I rang up the Town Hall to find out what proportion of my rates went on such vital things as holes and cleansing. It took the best part of three hours. One lady said crossly that I had a leaflet itemising such information sent to me every year with my rate demand. I said I'd lost it, and she said she'd send me another one, and I said why didn't she just get one out of the drawer and read it to me over the phone, and she said she had better things to do. I modified my tone and asked as politely as possible why she was being so unhelpful; she hung up. Did she feel in some way threatened by requests for details? Had she lost all the leaflets? Did she feel she was being asked to be more accountable than her wages warranted, or was it simply that she'd been frightened as a child by a snooty voice on the telephone?

Fortunately I then got through to a splendid young lady who was as interested as I was and eventually equally baffled. For instance, Camden spent £47,000 on road-mending this year. Think about it. Just pulling up my pavement, let alone the hundreds all over the borough, must have used up every penny. I thought that my hole must have cost at least

£30,000, not to mention the ones in Park Village East, and she explained that those were Gas Board holes, and that anyway residents in that street were getting 0.4 something or other off the rates for 'reduced amenities'. No, they couldn't sue the Gas Board for damages, but the day of reckoning was coming. I personally, she said, paid 77p a week to have my street swept and the pavements pulled up and down.

So there you are. All I have to do now is deduct 328p a month from my rates bill. The extra 20p is towards the mending of the heels on my shoes and the bandages I may need for my twisted ankles. I feel quite justified, and I suggest that anyone else who lives in a filthy, unswept area with the pavement surfaces rocking like see-saws should follow my example. Trouble is, I can't quite see who I'm getting at by taking such a step. There doesn't seem to be anybody out there who's accountable for the inefficiency and lack of service. Perhaps a private action brought against the gas board might be more satisfying, but then I'd have to fall down a hole and break a leg to get anywhere.

Never mind. See you in Holloway, unless something happens tomorrow.